Fiend

The Novel

Dr. F.

Cover Art: @Clitopatra

ISBN: 9798870359267

Table of Contents

Foreword

This isn't a manifesto nor an instruction manual on how to get away with the worst crime. This is a fictional account of what we all fear and want the most. To live in our own reality.

It is recommended that no one under the age of 18 reads this. The content in this book is beyond the limits for most. Therefore, the author is not responsible for any trauma that may be caused while experiencing this novel.

If you find yourself inclined to harm others, get help. If you attempt to contact the writer with illegal smut or proof of any harm toward anyone, all correspondence will be submitted to the authorities. Do not take this as a challenge but as a guarantee that the writer and publisher are not interested in real crimes.

This book was designed for the reading enjoyment of men. Some women will also enjoy the nuanced perspective taken. There aren't boundaries in here and all filters have been turned off. You have been warned.

If you're going to read this, it may be hard to smile in the future.

Prologue

The sky is grey, as it tends to be this half of the year in metro Detroit. Even at dawn, in November, this part of Michigan offers no anticipation to a brighter day. I've taken the 275 to my dump of a trailer park home, where nothing awaits me. It's adequately labeled as a dump because it's near a heap of trash south of 94 crammed between a landfill and train tracks. If I'm not being insulted by the foul smell of others' waste, or awoken at night by a freight train to carry goods to better people on the other side of the country, I'm being confronted by the drugs traded for sex by those in need. The highway provides a quick in and out into my community by outsiders looking for a fix to their problems.

But just as I pull off onto my exit and toward the aluminum shacks, to the right of my periphery, in the ravine, is a glare of blinking yellow light not in its right place. I've just come off a 12 hour volunteer shift at the fire station on a Sunday, hoping to get a solid 3 hours of shut eye before it's time to sit through another lecture on world history at Detroit college.

As my decrepit car pulls to the side of the road, I can hear screams and splashes of an individual or two climb over my blown out speakers. "Bodies" by Drowning Pool is on maximum volume. I grab my flashlight and window breaker I makeshifted out of a starter plug and steel clicky pen I found in a dumpster outside of an AutoZone.

It's a man with his boots out of the water diving for something under his vehicle now halfway toward Davey Jones' locker. Half of the back of his pickup truck is sticking out and the rear wheel is spinning dangerously fast in the open air.

I hop into Belleville Lake, but it's more of a sewage reservoir. The water seems cold. My feet are slow in here and my boots are adhering to the mud at the bottom. The old man is screaming hysterically, but I can't make out what he's saying. I'm too distracted by his missing teeth and saliva landing all over my face. I push him out of the way because he's more of a detriment to his passenger than any real assistance.

I dive face first and since I can't see who or what is lodged beneath, I need to feel my way around.

I return for air and I hear the belligerent man, "My boy is still buckled in! Please hel...!".

My face is again submerged in the cold murky water and I slide my hand along the slippery driver window. My trustworthy window-breaker bounces off the glass, but the window remains intact. Another piercing movement and this time my other hand feels the glass shatter underwater. The carbon dioxide inside my lungs is accumulating and starting to prick at my chest.

My boots barely make it through the small window of the pick-up and I feel a slightly colder body of tissue strapped into a seat. My free hand wraps almost all the way around it's small throat. Against my palm I detect a thready pulse, approximately 60 beats per minute, close to anoxia and eventual perish. I haven't felt the slow fading of life within my hands, but a child offers me no amusement.

The pocketknife in my back pocket slices the nylon seatbelt outward, de-strapping this small person. I grab it by the collar and start making my way out of the bleak city water.

I throw him above water and clutch him by the torso to walk toward the shore nearby. His father continues to show a hysterical reaction to the ordeal while helping me carry his child. I tell him to push on his chest and deliver compressions twice per second. But as expected he's too emotional to follow the simple task.

Paramedics from the local fire station arrive and take over. I walk away so I'm not taken down as an eyewitness. The father appears intoxicated and smells of liquor under his breath. He's blurting out "PLEASE" to the EMT's for them to resuscitate his boy.

As I open the door of my '96 Civic and begin removing the muddy boots before entering my smelly vehicle, I get a glimpse of water spitting out of the boy's mouth. Followed by tears and weeping by both parties. A stretcher is pulled out to take them away.

I can't believe I got fucking soaked for this shit.

It's too early for this melodrama. I have class at 10:15 am. It typically takes me 10 minutes to get home, and 5 minutes to get into bed.

Class is on Mondays, Wednesdays, and Fridays.

In between, I incorporate extracurricular diversions. Things to pass the time.

When god made me he was drunk. The devil delivered me.
My place of birth is purgatory. And hell is home.

Chapter 1

Predetermination

My name is Ryder Strickland and I'm a fiend to most things bad. I obsess and I persist on what most people in society would never accept.

There isn't much that I live for. I'm a simple man. I have a routine and I don't deviate from what I like. I like to see buildings on fire, I like to masturbate, and I like to absorb as much knowledge as possible.

I don't belong at the college, but it's a necessary step at leaving my forsaken station. I live alone in a 14 by 56 trailer home in the outskirts of Detroit.

I'm surrounded by black symbols. The writing on the wall are made of messages that I'm not alone. That I have some form of scope where I'm aiming my hostile intentions.

Breakfast consists of Ramen and a protein shake. Lunch is prepared on a propane hot plate where grilled cheese sandwiches take but a minute. And dinner is plated after opening a can of tuna.

I'm alone in this world. I never had anyone to care for me, and there isn't anyone to give a shit about. At 20 years old, I've learned from trial and error on how to survive in my set of circumstances.

If it takes a village to raise a child, then my village has done nothing but grant me the ability to be self-sufficient. From the very start of this journey those closest to me have harmed me. So why not return the favor onto those who are deserving?

#

Monday morning.

I've acclimated to dull routine. Doing the usual things to have a predictable pattern.

Sitting in the back of a lecture hall, my small laptop, purchased from a crackhead, is opened for taking notes. In the background is a media player playing back a video I downloaded. It's kink porn. Of a woman hanging upside down being doused with cold water and tased with a cattle prod. She's spread eagle and being pinched all over her sensitive areas with clothespins. Her clitoris and labia majora are fraught with pincers illustrating a circle of wooden pressure.

Her screams help me focus. With an earphone in my right ear, my left pays sufficient attention to capture the lesson presented by the ancient faculty at the podium.

In the row behind me is some younger girl, her stare is discernibly focused on the back of my head and whatever I'm doing on the computer. Fortunately the controls of the video playback are found on my keyboard and not on the screen for everyone behind me to see.

A light touch on my right shoulder distracts my divided attention, and when I turn, I inadvertently make contact with the grey in the iris of her piercing eyes. She has an intense gaze, as if she's pulling out information from inside me without my permission.

She asks, "How did you do on the last test?"

It was on Egyptian history and the Roman expansion. I fucking bombed it because the day earlier I responded to a two-story grease fire in meth country, and my breacher was out sick with the fucking flu.

"I think I got an 80." I don't know what emotion to signal in this type of situation.

She's fishing for information by attempting chit-chat.

"Better than me, I flunked it." She replies before I finish my sentence with a strange innuendo around the first letter of flunked.

She's acting slutty.

"You need a tutor". I respond prior to turning my back to her.

The professor glares at us, and I resume to burying my head in my laptop to pretend I'm taking notes. I raise the volume of the woman begging for the pain to stop. Her safety word is being ignored, just as I'm ignoring this girl's prying questions.

Careful with this one.

#

The class filled with impressionable minds could not have concluded soon enough. I'm the last to take my seat, and the first to leave the auditorium. On my way to the student parking lot, to find myself behind the wheel of my cramped rust box once again, I have to pass through the biology department.

Peering inside the vertical window, a glimpse of a freshman cutting into a piglet is caught in my periphery. The student barely out of prepubescence is slicing the abdomen open. They must be learning the anatomy of an organism and apparently the best way to do this is by feeling one's way around a small animal.

I have experience in this. He's doing it all wrong.

Regardless, I'm captivated and cannot lift my feet to leave this busy hallway. I can smell the formaldehyde from here. The utensil they're using, #11 scalpels, are reusable and likely dull to the touch by this point.

The novice professor should've went with the 15.

Which reminds me I need to replenish my stash. I hide a gym bag filled with equipment in the locker room at Gold's gym. For $10 a month I can work out the muscles necessary to ravish another human body and capable of carrying it long distances to discard it under approximately 5,000 pounds of undug dirt.

For a nominal gym membership fee I can also hide tools meant to bind, clean, slice, saw, and bury a large body of tissue. I've watched and read sufficient books with FBI agents as the main characters or written by FBI agents to learn that preparation is key.

I've purchased tools online using a gift card I purchased with cash at a local corner store. The items are delivered to a P.O. box I rent at a florist which doubles as a UPS location that I know doesn't have any cameras installed. This part of town is quite barren but one can never be too careful as federal agents have proven ways to follow digital and paper trails.

Within my duffel bag held in a locker secured by a dial padlock, are several carefully selected items. A 10-foot single cotton rope for binding limbs, tape for strapping a mouth shut, pliers in case teeth need to be removed, a zippo lighter for starting a flame, a 10x monocular to spot a doe, a dog whistle to distract a woman's bestfriend, a stainless steel diving knife, and a foldable shovel that doubles as a handsaw for thick branches of flesh.

I haven't killed a person, yet.

But when I'm ready, I'm confident that success will result at my moment of most inspiration.

I've already mapped out multiple locations within the city, in the bowels of the most rundown neighborhoods. Inside these abandoned homes, dirt flooring is easily found under a thin layer in which I can quietly dig a large enough hole. Other locations include deserted factory buildings where dumpsters have been forgotten with flammable debris already inside. I've collected and placed large steel plates nearby to enclose a fire so it can reach 1000 plus degrees Celsius. This way the bones are immolated without the fire spreading to the actual building structure.

We all need hobbies, and this is my form of entertainment. Some people prepare for doomsday, as I make provisions to bring about the apocalypse for a special person.

To err is divine, but to hurt is sublime.

Chapter 2

Seize and Resist

A worthwhile way to spend one's time is in the pursuit of happiness.

Unfortunately, I don't recognize that particular emotion nor others. I can feel excitement evidenced by adrenaline spiking my body temperature. I can detect lust and horniness by the pulsated gorging of my dickhead. I can even become acutely aware of anger when my left hand begins to tremor. But joy is not a sensation with which I'm familiar.

I wish we would experience fear more recurrently.

Instead I find myself chasing the sensation that trickles the dopamine down the back of my neck. I've always wondered if that's where dopamine originates from because when I'm on the hunt, as I like to call it, the hairs on the back of my neck rise and noticeably vibrate. They initiate locomotion throughout my body and I cannot sit still.

When I'm driving around town and looking for a prospect, my mind goes blank and my eyesight becomes keenly focused on the particular prey for which I'm athirst.

My hearing becomes attuned to sounds that are pertinent to my prey, obfuscated to noise pollution not serving any purpose. God forbid I smell comforting perfume or sweet lotion on a passing bag of skin, as my olfactory nerves will send me into a mindfucking craze. I once followed a woman for three days memorizing her daily routines from dawn to dusk.

That was a much needed shower at the end, after sweating and playing with myself in the car throughout the hunt.

I didn't make a move because I was dispatched to a fire in a neighboring town where their local fire station was attending to another incident.

What I feel on most days is boredom. I struggle with twiddling my thumbs and sitting on my hands when there's so many beautiful victims walking around. This desire to hurt others, especially women, prevents me from being normal.

I wasn't taught how to love or less how to maintain any relationship. I don't have any friends and I've never dated. What I do know is how to find people.

At the firehouse I'm a better search and rescue than Rascal, the fucking dalmatian. I don't mind the heat or putting myself in cramped spaces. All I need is a pickaxe to burrow through a home that's hot as hell. And just like the canine, it's the act of seeking not discovery that sets me off. My proverbial bone is the body, conscious or not, that I grab and fireman carry out of any precarious scenario.

It's Tuesday and I have my volunteer hat on. When at the firehouse, I only step inside Engine 33 when on official duty. When I walk in, no one greets me. It's as if I'm invisible, which I certainly prefer. Whenever the team is receiving a mandatory briefing I stand in the back away from anyone's focus. I'm just here to expend some energy and learn a skill or two.

On my way out back to my daily routine, the Chief garners my attention, "Strickland, you're coming up on your first probationary year. Are you caught up on your continued education?".

"Not quite sir. I'm studying for the EMS cert." I try to obviate being given more work.

"Once you're ready, let me know and we'll get you to the Firefighter II school."

"Roger, sir. Thank you." I about-face and get out of dodge as quickly as possible.

The volunteer job, that I hold until the degree is completed, is a distraction because no one should hunt every day. For one, it would raise too many alarms and engage a statewide investigation about the attacks. Secondly, I presume it would cause my mental health to slip deeper into a state of derealization.

I've been there before.

#

The actual catalyst to losing my sanity three years ago was an elusive target that I tracked for about a week.

As my mother's custody was called into question, I left home in a haste after fulfilling the requisite credits for a high school diploma. On my way out of school to pick up my degree certificate, the guidance counselor requested an exit interview since I decided to skip out on graduation.

That one was an endearing woman with delightful physical attributes. An English accent is belling in my ear.

She was a lot younger than her peers as a fresh college graduate and only a few years older than me. One of the few adults at the time that treated me with a semblance of courtesy with care in her big blue eyes. Her toenails were pedicured, tipped in a thick white that reminded of Headlands Beach in Ohio. I visited once when my mother and I escaped her abusive boyfriend for a weekend.

Plus, she smelled like the samples at the entrance of Bath and Body Works. Where families seemed to congregate and exchange jovial remarks as they tested new scents onto each other. It was nauseating to watch from the food court, ruining my fucking dinner.

Her smell, coupled with her considerate smile, and wild blonde hair had me in a trance of attraction. I couldn't help myself around her.

I waited for her in the faculty parking lot as she walked in her cork-wedged heels to her Mini Cooper. I followed her to yoga class and sat patiently in my mother's half-broken sedan as I feasted my eyes on her stretch poses. I watched over her on a dinner date through the restaurant window as she ate across from a well-built man in a suit. I tailed her to her two story townhome and memorized the combination she used on the attached garage underneath her living room. When she was at school, I once rummaged through her belongings taking several pairs of underwear that I would wear around my neck while I slept.

I would park at a gas station next to her rental community. To avoid the cameras at the entrance of her neighborhood, I jumped a chain link fence with ease. I had a late growth spurt, as my neighbor would say to me, and at that age I'd already reached my determined height of 5 foot 11.

At the time I carried no equipment, but I furnished a curiosity that would take me inside her most intimate space. Watching her during somnolence, from the balcony that opened into her bedroom, was a past time I most enjoyed. I don't think most people realize how facile it is to climb pretty much any structure, especially with the aid of a large windowsill and low hanging fruit where the railings are easy to grab hold of.

I was able to hide behind a wall that provided cover to the right of her sliding glass door. Her bedroom faced the back of the neighborhood adjacent to a large oak tree and nothing else. The only person looking out for her, peering at her small chest as she respirated during deep sleep, was me with my face against the dusty screen covering the piece of glass dividing her from the rest of the world.

I tried opening the sliding patio door every night, but I never caught a lucky break. I likely would have had my way with her body if it was ever left unlocked. The loud garage would have alerted her, so I didn't consider that as well. I masturbated to her live body in front of me for three nights in a row and purposefully ejaculated against the glass in high hopes she would notice and test it by rubbing her perfect fingers against it.

On the fifth night, she brought home the well-dressed man into her home after a painstakingly dull date at the county fair. I didn't have the cash to cover the entrance fee, so I jumped this slightly taller fence near where the carnies made their mobile homes. Their date together was cheesy like the chick-flicks I'd study on my 24 inch flatscreen tv. This asshole won her an oversized stuffed animal and forced her to carry it throughout the park.

So I decided to beat him to the punch and be at the ready on her second story patio prior to their arrival. Hiding behind my favorite wall so I can break the glass with a brick I kept for this type of emergency.

They showered together which caused my foot to shake and left hand to tremble. I watched her undress in front of him without awareness that I was just outside, with the hardest dick I've ever felt.

Just as I was turning the brick to its sharp edge out, to break the glass door down in a single hit, this motherfucker walks right toward me. He has something in his hand, what appeared to be a lighter and small cigarette joint. Right at the last second before he approached the mortise lock and struggled to unlatch it, I vanished into the hidden corner of the concrete terrace. I already figured he saw me. But right when he opened the inevitable sliding door to face me like a man, I raised the hard clay above my head and dropped it with everything I had.

This asshole also raised his hand in synchrony, almost out of reflex, and blocked my clay hammer. At first all was quiet, but this pussy started screaming for her.

His screechy voice raised "Sam! SAM!! Someone is..!!!".

Again, I tried to punch him with the short end of the block right toward his stupid face, without saying a word.

But he was quicker than anticipated, wasn't he?

In the furthest corner of my eye I noticed the yellow of her head poke past her bathroom door.

And simultaneously as I threw another punch, he ducked out of the way and the weight of my thrust landed me on his right shoulder. And with a simple football style technique he defensively rushed me against the railing of the heightened structure. My back cracked the bolts holding it in place to the cemented foundation, and I rolled backwards right off her second floor.

Fortunately I landed on my side with just the inner wind knocked out of me. I can still hear her screaming.

"Oh my god, Rick!!" She squeaked, "WHAT'S GOING ON???"

And as I stood to regain my disrespected composure, I saw her bright blue eyes, illuminated by the moon and augmented streetlight… they meet mine. I was still in view under the lamps and was able to capture her jaw drop as I scurried my weakened feet away.

That was humiliating.

And out of self-redemption I considered the very next logical thing to do. Going home to my compact trailer home was not an option in case the authorities search for me at the location recorded inside my school record.

I was fucking infuriated and livid for what he did to me. I remember snarling with saliva shooting from my mouth in so much vexation as I drove circles around town.

#

Like a message from above, as I avoided going home after being thrown off the balcony, I was reminded of who started me on this dark trek: godforsaken Mr. and Mrs. Beck. The ones that forced me to watch my mother get railed over the years. What's more, as their employer they thought it best to contact the authorities on her behalf after learning of her instability.

This all happened when I was 17, right after my mother was sent away. What did I do after the disgraceful, failed attack? I went and attacked that married couple that did Mother wrong. I beat them to a pulp for everything they did to her. The assault took place while they were strapped to the seats of their luxury vehicle.

I waited for what seemed hours outside of their gated community in my vehicle carrying a full erection, after the patio incident. I followed them as they left, and found the right time to sneak into their car while they dropped off their precious daughter to a late movie.

The attack took place in a restaurant parking lot. A two-course meal from the drive-through. Devoured, but made a mess.

I lived out of my car for several weeks after all of this. Either no one contacted the cops or they didn't have enough eyewitness to I.D. me as the perp. Nor is there a database of semen to analyze the ejaculate I deposited while punching Mrs. Beck in the chest and over her abdomen. With one hand on my cock and one hand beating her senseless.

Nevertheless, I allowed my lustful aggression to take control and land me in a state of constant paranoia watching over my shoulder for the onrush of police to take me in. That lasted for several months.

Never again.

That was 36 months ago, and the embarrassment felt by being man-handled was not at all absolved by pounding on the two pounds of flesh. Beating an older couple did nothing for me because they were defenseless and worthless.

I've since learned to be more proactive in choosing my victims; not for what they did to me, but for who they are.

Maiming the innocent is safer then exacting revenge. What would seem random selection is a guise to throw off the scent to anyone making sense of what I do.

How good am I if all it takes is a novice detective to line up a victim profile on a chalk board to figure out what I'm about?

We're not living in high cotton. We're pricking our fingers on the bolls. For a dollar of nothin'. In his debt ever more.

Chapter 3

Penny For Your Thoughts

Finding sustenance is an endeavor for which I've been responsible alone since I can remember. Even before mother was sent away, she was neglectful at best and inhuman on most days. So food and water, as I learned from an early age, is a requirement I cannot ignore or I'll end up in the ICU with a feeding tube down my nose again.

Failure to thrive has been a repeat statement in my medical chart since my youngest age.

I find myself always hungry except for when I'm hunting. It's as if the fear of others suppresses my own natural needs. Something about feeling the physiological stress of an animal under my weight fills me.

On most days, tuna and Ramen will only go so far. The need to stalk and slash is a craving I'm tormented with as long as I'm awake.

I cannot recall the last time I've had a full meal. I refuse to step into a soup kitchen surrounded by those putrid smelling individuals. I'm talking about the staff as well as the patrons. Stepping into a church for me is like a mouse being baited into a trap. Sure, a scrap of food is enticing but at what cost.

The Dollar General is my supermarket. Where I can pick up an item or two at a time to satiate my hunger.

In the middle of the week, on a Wednesday afternoon, something to get me through the rest is imperative. I used to forget, but now I have an alarm set on my phone.

Today, a box of instant noodles, high fructose soda pop, and Chicken of the Sea are in my basket. I've covered my daily requirement of carbs, glucose, and protein for caloric intake. All within my $5 a day to feed a person in need. And I need to stay awake to evade The Board at night.

They're most present when I sleep. So I make it almost a daily habit to hit the processed food aisle.

Today the girl at the cash register recognizes me and waves me over to check out. I haven't noticed until today that her name tag reads: Aria. I can't help myself but examine the tattoo covering her left cleavage. It's a childish name of someone close to her: Aiden.

She asks me, "Hey, how are you today?"

"Fine," I react.

"Same old food, huh?", she probes.

I don't say a word but stare at the cheap belt embracing the space above her curvaceous buttocks.

She's naturally tanned and could pass for either Black or of Latin ethnicity. Her lips are like inflatable tubes that kids use at the pool. Her eyes big and endearing when she looks at me. Her hair is perfectly arranged with swirls that vine down her light brown temples. She put forth effort in her appearance prior to showing up at her employment today, as she has every time I've seen her.

She would make the perfect meat-sleeve for a dick. A country accent bounces in my head.

But I can't be so foolish to consider her as my next victim. She knows my face and the cameras have recorded my pattern at this location for months.

The greenscreen on the cash register rings up $5.15. Fuck, I'm short 15¢. And I haven't eaten in two days.

I can pay for food or I can leave my car here as I've been on empty for three days.

The white in my eyes must be showing because her eyebrows raised immediately after noticing mine.

"Honey, it's ok. Just go ahead".

In such few words, she has fed me for today.

"Uhh." I don't know what to say. My feet aren't moving.

"Just get out of here, I got you." She smiles and it confuses the shit out of me.

No one has ever got me.

#

She reminds me so much of a young girl I once knew. The daughter of my mother's employers. A girl innocent and uncorrupted surrounded by a world of vulgarity and harsh adults.

She's innocent in the sense that she isn't familiar with the immorality of man. She may have grown up here and seen some shit, but her eyes don't emit suffering. She hasn't been broken. One can sense when a person's spirit has been fractured from their sense of self. She spoke to me with kindness that wasn't altruistic or charitable. It was decent.

Her soul has yet to have been corrupted. She doesn't start her day to take advantage of others. A person like her may care about herself, as she clearly did her physical appearance, but doesn't find the need to remove from others to serve herself.

Physically, she resembled nothing to the young girl of my earlier life. But her gentleness mirrored that of a child that at one time distracted me of the events that took place around us.

#

On my short drive home, the thought of what she did has not stopped circling in my mind.

Why would anyone risk their livelihood for a complete stranger? A woman's voice pings into my ears.

She risked losing her job over 15 cents. Or worse that she would spend her money on feeding someone unimportant to her. Who the fuck does that?

Is she looking for a way of making me owe her? The danger she just placed herself in for making someone like me owe her. I could kill her over less than a quarter and not think twice.

Who the fuck is Aiden?

#

I stop at a gas station on the way home. Convening out front are several degenerate men with treachery in their eyes. They always have some shit to say.

"Hey boy! Come here! Let me holla at ya!"

My mind is still spinning about what she did, and I barely hear them.

I only have enough to fill $2 worth of gas and purchase an overpriced box of cigarettes. I hand the clerk $6 in one dollar bills.

Standing behind me is a belligerent nuisance cursing over his breath, too close for my comfort.

"This punk bitch holdin' up the line with your cheap ass gas!"

I turn around to get a better look of what his soul is made of. His eyes are drooping and crossed.

Don't cause a scene here, Ryder. They'll call the cops. She warns.

"The fuck you starin' at, boy!?"

I return my focus on the exchange of cash for goods. The clerk obliges to hand over the pack of Newport menthols. He has an anxious look on his face, the type of look that a grown man has when he's about to be robbed.

I turn my body to get close to the intoxicated man's ear.

Lad, don't let one instigator rile up your behavior. The British professor warns.

Rip his fuckin' head off! The farmhand incites.

"Can I speak to you outside for a moment?"

"Aw hell! This motherfucker wants to see some shit!"

Other patrons inside the gas station start laughing and provoke him to escalate the situation.

This is not the place nor the time, my dear! The lady in my head raises her voice.

I walk out with the pack in my pocket. I walk through the group meeting outside, while loudmouth is calling out insults.

"Ya'll want to see some shit! This bitch wants to have words!" More individuals cheer the inebriated man, venting foul air out of their mouths.

I lead him to behind the building followed by the gang of observers.

Once out of the streets, and right when the man stands with his fists raised, I walk straight at him.

"Let's go motherfucker! I'm gonna teach you something!" He yells loud enough for everyone watching to hear him.

Ryder, do not kill him. Control yourself please. Now she's being unusually nice to me.

But right as he finishes his menacing sentence, I fake an overhand right, and follow with a straight left into his Adam's apple.

He wheezes and tries to gulp a gallon of air. But it won't work since I felt his windpipe collapse against my middle knuckle.

He's holding his throat with both hands looking at the ground with the white in his eyes showing wide. That's not the best form to protect oneself. I put him out of his misery with a right knee up his snotty nose. He's dropped and falls on his back. Blood is gushing out of both nostrils.

"OOHH! HHEYY!" His group of cowering gentleman disapprove of the attack on their brother.

I walk toward them again, just as they've asked of me moments before.

They make way. No one halts my pace as I look into the faces of as many vagabonds in the steps it takes me to return to the front of the store.

I pump my gas without a worry that I'll be bothered again today.

My mind doesn't stay with them long. I'm back on the pretty girl at the dollar store.

#

Within the sanctuary of my four vinyl walls, inside this small trailer home, dollar store girl is living rent free in my head. For pennies on the dollar.

Nighttime has arrived. And my imagination gets louder in the absence of sunlight.

Her lips would probably feel phenomenally soft at the base of my cock if throat fucked until completion. Her ass likely spreads beyond comparison if a tongue were buried within it. Those breasts of hers are small enough to palm in one hand and squeeze tight enough to rip them off. I wonder if she's ever been choked before, or had her hair pulled back. I contemplate if her father used to spank her when she broke the rules.

After dropping off my pathetic groceries on a counter beside the single hot stove, my pants are lowered to my ankles. I plop my ass in a recliner with a rag waiting on the armrest.

Her fruity smell is still infused in my nostrils and serves as inspiration while I stroke my dick up and down. I use my own spit for lubrication. Her voice is echoed in my ears while I wrap the shaft with one grip and rub my head with the other. I'm imagining her small hands replace mine as I pull on my dick with 10 fingers, up and down. Her eyes are imbedded into my eyes shut tight at the very moment ejaculate shoots past my seated position and lands on the hard floor in front of me. It's oozing down my knuckles and dripping over my balls. My body is contracted with every muscle tense as I envision her soft skin being rubbed. Her imagined taste is being licked off my lips while the semen is rubbed into the skin around my shaft.

What sort of freak would jack off to that!

The kind that knows no better.

The crusty rag suffices to wipe my genitals and hands clean. But the viscid fluid is only smeared and now crusty to the touch.

I fall asleep in the same position. Without the need to thoroughly clean myself, I allow the bleak moment of satisfaction splash over my body. Air drying any sentiment of longing for others, to become keenly aware of the rising tide of hostility's return.

Being under their spell is a state of anxiety.
Calamity their native dialect. Insanity being the dwelling.

Chapter 4

The Debates and Discourse Alliance

During somnolence, The Board sounds off their thoughts on the matter.

The voice that I recognize as the English professor is at the forefront. *Shouldn't you make use of her body instead of availing oneself to such gestures?*

A second member, the arrogant farmer chimes in. *Ain't much sense to spend yer own instead of spilling hers.*

The voice I'm most apprehensive about speaks the most. She's a snake who hisses her influence into me. *I don't think you care about her, so what do you care if she's cut down?*

I respond in my dream, "I can't touch her. You all know that."

Who said anything bout touchin'... His twang rings in my head.

Just think how much you'd enjoy ripping her in half. She rasps close to my internal ear.

"But I go there once a week, I would be the first person of interest." I try to reason with insanity.

The professor redirects my concern. *My boy, you know that within this neighborhood everyone is of interest.*

There's no harm in following her around. You would so enjoy that. You know that. She has a way of forcing me into things.

I rebut "And if she spots me? That would be it, I wouldn't be able to go back."

You can do as you please. The professor reminds me.

And if she makes you, there's other dollar stores in town. Don't be so cataclysmic. Medusa speaks.

"Let's say I capture her, what's my plan? I have the station and college six days a week." The logistics are laid out.

I'm sure we would keep her busier than a two-dollar trollop on nickel night. The southerner declares.

We could keep her locked tight while you go on about your day. She sibilates her threats.

"And let me guess, fuck her repeatedly when I return? For how long?"

As long as you'd like ol' chap.

An eccentric member of The Board rarely vocalizes himself and only when things get serious.

He's the voice of reason. *Maybe wait and see if this is the right one.*

The fucking farmer again. *That ain't much of a plan now is it!*

Let him come to his own conclusions. She-snake tries to charm me again.

“This is reckless..” I plea for logical thought.

But now they’re arguing amongst themselves and I’m the rope being tugged upon.

The logical one has a deep voice. *If he’s not ready he’s apt to make a mistake. And we do not want that.*

Mistakes can be costly, but he won’t be the one to pay! His drawl is getting agitated.

We’ll protect you Ryder, as we always have.. The female snake charmer again.

Ol’ boy I think you’re more afraid of yourself than of the consequences. His proper English makes me feel like I’m his property.

“I don’t know…” I truly do not know.

And my eyes open and there I am. Standing with my pants down not being supported anymore by the cushions of the seat. Drenched in sweat. I wipe the beads of perspiration off my brow and try to shake the streams falling down my chest.

#

The last time I listened to The Board they convinced me to attack a woman walking her dog at night.

I was driving through Grosse Point looking around for my type. Precarious is what I was. A boy easily influenced by his demons and horny beyond comparison.

These upscale communities are not on edge about safety as much as the urban areas. They’re quiet and unsuspecting. Especially not expecting an 18-year-old boy at the time, with my skin color, to commit any heinous crime.

Once the prospect was spotted I parked my car in a dark parking lot and walked around until I saw her from afar again.

The Board were all talking, simultaneously, giving me instruction on what to do next. Each with its own plan of attack and all wanting the same outcome.

Repeating phrases like *take her, grab her and run, tackle her*. Synchronizing the words *stick it inside her*.

Until the deafening commands drove me past my limits and carried my feet behind hers. I was trailing from a negligent distance not making a single sound of feet scuffling the pavement.

I walked quietly behind her. A woman in her late 30's being pulled by a small terrier. I was wearing a black shirt with sweatpants and a backwards hat so as to appear like a guy who belonged. But a guy at the ready to unclothe or run if needed.

Parallel to the sidewalk on which we strolled was a tree line bordering Palmer Park. A heavy brush without any observable light allowed in.

Both of her ears were plugged with earphones and her right arm was strapped to an exercise phonecase. She walked in her own world without concern that anything could ever happen to her.

Not even her dog picked up my scent as a light breeze against our direction pushed me further back. But I could hear her humming to her playlist and gyrating her almost perfect ass with every step.

From this far behind I can still see her wedding ring glisten in the moon's light. A stone being waved like a statement that she is loved. At her age I also assumed she had children.

In full sprint I tackled her from the back. Taking her small body to the concrete ground. With such force that her voice was lost and the earbuds fell out. As we landed partly on her miniature dog, it ran off out of fear that its master had been intercepted and obliterated without forewarning.

The Board cheered in my head after the replay-worthy take down had taken place. Like a choir chanting: *drag her, take her, pull her to the woods*.

I wrapped myself around her waist and covered her mouth with my hand, lifting her flaccid body away from the concrete path. Then, as she was regaining her bearings she began fighting and reaching to pull her body away from my bear hug. She tried to bite my hand. Even scratching my arm quite badly with the sharpened stone, alarming me to control her better. Requiring me to hold my pointer and middle fingers over her nostrils to control the muffled screams.

But it was too late for her. We had already found a patch off the beaten path. Away from anyone who may be walking nearby and lend a helping hand.

And The Board was already in action to solicit advice on how to make it happen.

Rip her pants off. The woman's voice.

Take them off, boy. I distinctly remember his accent changed to Irish or Scottish or whatever.

I stood over her to pull her spandex past her ankles. Removing her sneakers with it in one swift tug. Manhandling her small legs so as to not let her defend against my assault.

She began begging and crying while folding her legs, and crab crawling into thicker brush. She forced me to jump on her chest.

The Board approved: *smack her, choke her out son, don't let'er go.*

My knife's blade folded out and was pressed against her neck. I didn't expect her to know what her carotid meant to me so I laid it on her breathing tube instead. She froze like a statue in mid-motion. Glaring into my eyes for mercy.

Slice her neck it'll make this quicker.

But instead I pulled out my obelisk cock and slowly found the hole that caused all this trouble. Holding her wrists with my other hand above her head and compressed into the sticks beneath.

"Oh my god, Oh my god, Jesus Christ." She cried quietly to herself.

Thataboy.

Superb.

Her cries still turn me on when heard in my nightmares.

"No, please no, please, please please!" she implored.

I thrusted for several moments while her thighs parted lifelessly and rocked with me. Her forearms trembled in my grip while she winced with every jab of my hips. Her face quaked side to side as sweat dripped off my face and into her mouth.

The heat between us caused me to perspire and struggle to maintain my grasp of the situation.

I can remember the sensation of her skin being gashed as clear as if it happened today. As I ejaculated into her suburban pussy, the left hold I had around her wrists broke apart and made me fall over her. My chest slammed into her chest. And the serrated blade I was mistakenly holding tense slid out of my right hand.

The act of trying to regain my grab of the rubber handle caused me to slash her cheek on the right side of her face.

She didn't initially make any sound, likely out of shock of what she just heard. The ripping of tight skin and carving motion into her jawbone.

I got up quite quickly from the surprise and saw what I had sawed.

Her two dirty hands held over her skin flap and she begun to roll around in the mud.

Squealing like a stuck pig, "EEEEH, OH MYY GAAH!!"

As I stood there watching the scene unfold my dick was still leaking and spilling into the pants wrapped around my socks.

You did good sweetheart. Now grab your things and go. A woman's voice alerted me.

Don't forget yer shoes. Country man assists.

Or the bloody knife! Professor almost scolds.

At first I sprinted right into the sidewalk like a child, but quickly jogged my own memory that I cannot call on any attention after all that.

I walked as slow as my legs allowed me to my car, and took my time with the door. I made it out of the park and even used my turn signal because…safety first.

#

So to say that The Board has always steered me in the right direction would be aggrandizing their purpose.

They're self-serving, and although they live inside me I know I'm not always in their best interest.

I don't care if they're aware of my introspection. They know that I know.

And because I know they're dangerous entities, lately that makes them more audacious. They push me to behave in ways that are not cautious, but carefree of what is likely to happen.

#

It's fucking morning again. Another day another struggle.

Keeping my head leveled and not off into the deep end is a full time job. Keeping them at bay while they espouse their fucking comments all god damn day is exhausting.

During my ice cold shower of water barely sprinkling the soap off me, taking with it my stress, The Board initiates their harassment again.

She won't be missed. No one will ever know. She whispers out of the blue.

It's the logical next step in a young man's life. Professor lectures.

"Is it?", I question.

For some it is... The rational baritone vibrates inside.

I try to spray the water into my ear to deafen the sound of their voices, but it's internal. What a stupid attempt.

You can't block us out now, ya know that! The hillbilly yells.

"I'm not trying to block you out, I just need to think." I bargain for a moment of silence.

Think?! You don't think! She snarls in my head.

Ol' boy, we do the thinking for you.

Can't and never could, don't ferget that!

"I just don't want to rush this. It's dangerous." I beg for some more time.

Time is of the essence in these matters. The low pitch voice throws me off.

"But if I mess up I…"

You never believe in yourself. She interrupts.

You need to trust us. We know what we're doing. The academic rings in again.

"I do trust you but can't I pick someone else?"

It has to be her! She growls louder this time.

I told y'all he's chicken shit. He don't have it!

"I'm not scared of anything!! I'm just not going to rot in a jail cell. In a cage like Mother!" I bark back.

Is that a self-fulfilling prophecy? The deep voice questions my self-belief.

"Of course not." I know what I can do.

I catch a glimpse of myself pacing against the hazy aluminum kettle.

Then why not just try your best? The professor resounds.

Ain't like you done stole nothin'. She ain't even here yet.

Just follow her around, darling.

"No." I stand my ground.

No?! The hick snaps back.

What do you really want. The baritone voice speaks up.

"I need to do my own thing. Without any help!" I try to push them back.

We're only here to guide you. She tries to soothe me down.

Quit bein' ugly. You ain't shit without us. Fucking redneck.

"I don't give a fuck! Leave me alone." I'm not budging on this one.

I'm standing in front of my front door with my fists clenched tight. Without any clothes on. And staring at nothing.

One doesn't realize when selfishness prevents one from living. The Englishman tries to sermonize to me.

He'll come crawlin' back. Like a mutt with his tail between his legs.

I don't crawl for anyone. Nor rest on my knees. If I need them it'll be to find my way into the darkness.

But my self-preservation is the most important, and not without clear thought. Especially when they're disconcerted like this and leading me into a hazardous scene.

I don't trust them, and they know that.

Being heated by the warmth is a ruse.
The smoke at the chimney untrue.
Losing oneself, falling through a trench of refuse.

Chapter 5

Controlled Chaos

Nighttime in Detroit is my comfort. It's a place quiet but loud at the same time.

Others are out with their kindred spirits, but I'm either out scoping, stalking, or simulating my next act.

I can hear laughing, loud calling out to each other, even at times quarrelling amongst themselves. These citizens need each other.

But I'm not one of them. I'm on an island of one. Singular in respect with whom I interact. Talking only to myself.

I'm absorbed within me and focused on what I like to do. And that is creating destruction inconspicuously without calling attention.

I can't do these things, attacking women or lighting buildings on fire, in broad daylight. Cameras and eyewitnesses would easier track my appearances under the bright sun. Instead the absence of light is my refuge where I can enter and vanish as much as I'd like.

Tonight I'm returning to a neighborhood which I've watched for hours inside my disagreeable front seat. It's a black community. Also more active before dawn as I am.

The building I've favored is nestled between two rundown houses away from the commotion of music and intoxication. An American-Foursquare house with two stories in between a couple of bungalows. The surrounding residences are pitch dark. It was once a well-blueprinted home filled with class, but it's now tinder meant to be burned down. The structure is boarded with plywood over the windows, and a white piece of paper is nailed to the front door written with: Notice Of Eviction.

Igniting a property ablaze induces a sensation of control painted with boldness. A form of assertion onto the landscape that will result in only one thing; ruin. Turning a carefully designed piece of art, like a woman, into a scorched pile of ash is not only sexually deviant but sadistically delicious. A way of humiliating not only its architect but its owner.

I have a zippo lighter in my right pocket and a 12 ounce can of lighter fuel inside my sweater pouch. But this home will require little to no fuel depending on the source of my flaming.

Last time I was here the back door had its locked removed by yours truly. Wonders what the handle of a shovel will do to a doorknob. My foldable shovel also serves for a makeshift crowbar on an old wooden door frame.

A mattress upstairs with several upholstered chairs and nightstands on top of it will be my oversized kindling. A bonfire will be established on the second story, causing a rapid spread to the other rooms upstairs. The bathtub in the master downstairs holds a carpet rolled up to engulf the lower floor of the house. The hipped roof above should make for glorious height in the flames as it's arched by long wooden beams.

Instead of spraying the lighter fluid all onto the mattress, I line a trail to lead the fire into the hallway. And branch it into the other rooms, making an easy track of polymer fibers and oxygen, into the children's rooms for the fire to consume. I know they're children's rooms because its fucking obvious with dolls laid out.

I flip the zippo over and pull on the flint wheel. A spark and a flame is all it takes to light the corner of the mattress while holding the lighter half an inch away. What started as a flickering glow in the unilluminated room, quickly turned into a scratching inferno before me.

The cloth cushion on the chairs burn first and spread onto the wooden furniture around them. Hell on earth in-house where they once dwelled; some fucking family.

The heat spread so fast and into the other rooms like a cat in heat looking for its mate, that I had to find my way out as expeditiously as possible.

But the mattress burned straight through, past its coils, and relinquished the support beneath it. Scorching a hole in the wore down floorboards under it, dropping the entire bonfire onto the first floor. The bedroom on the second floor is left with a sizzling puncture, like a twisted poker which has been stabbed into the hide of a dead animal. All within what feels like seconds to minutes of initiation.

I'm racing to find my way out of the enlightened room because I can feel the hot temperature to my sides and underneath.

The stairs at the end of the hallway are torched like the steps to Hades' underworld. The rooms at the other end have begun to torch. The only direction of less hellfire is the one in which I was just in.

Without hesitation, out of self-perseveration, I jump over the gaping hole and keep my momentum as I run through the glassless window with just a piece of cardboard blocking the moonlight from entering the room.

My error in judgment, and miscalculation of threat versus reward, has lead me to jump through a thick glass as dirty as the board over it. The glass was intact prior to my exit, but broke entirely once my body passed through.

My body bounced off the first story roof and crashed on the wore down grass to the side. I laid there a moment to self-triage my sustained injuries, with nothing incapacitating found. Just a nice gash into my right forearm, into my muscle where the white meat shows.

After wrapping my bleeding arm in the sweater I'm wearing by tying a double knot, I found a clearance far from the danger of crackling walls and snapping furniture. Re-adjusting the cotton tourniquet as tight as possible.

My pocket vibrates and chimes an incoming call.

Who the fuck is calling you…

"Ryder, this is Engine 34. We've got a Code 3, and we're calling all volunteer responders to Claytown at 6118 30th Street. Can you confirm your ETA?"

The very house of our choosing.

"I'm on my way. I'll be about 10 minutes." This is going to be an ironic encounter.

I back up to my vehicle and pull out a smoke, to be broken out in emergencies. A menthol Newport that gets sucked into my lungs quicker than the incinerating roof.

From a distance, afar from the crowd compiling around the residence consumed in yellow, is a fire truck spinning its alarm and red lights for everyone to see and hear.

I sit on the hood of my car, with it turned on, to heat up the engine and surface covering it, enjoying the fuck out of this nicotine stick. Covering possible evidence that I've been here for a while.

The collection of underprivileged community members begin to swarm the street before the burning house.

The fire engine slams its brakes ahead of the crowd, not being able to park in front of the hydrant on the sidewalk, so it stops a house or two away. The team of highly trained professionals set up shop in their predetermined roles, as I slowly walk over to the loud truck. The team lead, who I recognize as my first instructor at the academy, and I make eye contact. I remember his face because right after introducing himself he pulled out a Polaroid of his entire 7-person family. To remind me of what's waiting back for us. I found it comical because nothing and no one has ever waited for me.

He points at the cabin at the front of the truck to get me started.

"Ryder get yourself dressed, let's go son!"

I throw on a jacket, helmet, and gloves, with no time for fire retardant pants. They won't be getting any of this gear back.

The younger guy on the team tugs on the water hose and a second in command is already wrenching on the screw sitting on the head of the hydrant far away. The team sergeant, is walking toward the door of the house with an ax in hand as he's opening the valve to his oxygen tank.

"Ryder, check in with the fellas by the pump!" He commands before hacking at the door.

He's a man on a bloody mission, innit'.

I'm surprised he remembers my name. It's a three man team of giants standing on each other's shoulders.

To the second fireman, I call out my home station of origin, "Hey, I'm from Engine…" to which I'm ignored and yelled at to check the back door for any survivors who have found their exit.

"Check the back, motherfucker!"

I do as I'm told because I need to stay out of the way. They can't become aware of what I just did.

And as I'm checking the unbared backdoor for a non-existent survivor, the youngest smoke jumper runs past my back.

"Where the fuck is Sergeant Briggs!" He doesn't slow down to deliver his message, but keeps searching for the officer in-charge.

And in the slowest frame of vision, a gust of wind picks up a handful of kindling over the gap between the homes and lands them on the property next door.

We both look up in awe of what we're watching, what we're expecting to happen next.

It first lands on the roof which doesn't extinguish but instead sources the fire on its flammable material. The flame quickly travels through the wooden ceiling and falls into the home. Like an ember falling on paper.

The crowd begins screaming. No one ran to the house next door to warn anyone of the impending doom nearby.

A woman screams.

"They still in there!" She cries out.

My arm is throbbing and blood is beginning to pool inside my glove.

The youngest Jake calls out to me, "Get the fuck in there and look for Sergeant Briggs!"

Both of them are sprinting right into the next house urgently through different openings. Bumping and crashing into walls making way for their oversized bodies.

I slowly open the backdoor and walk into black fog. With no haste to my step.

I call out his name.

"Sarg! Sergeant Briggs!! Where are you?"

There's a large amount of smoke, and a ball of fire that's climbing the ceiling. It's coming from the left side of the house what looks like the living room. It looks like hell upside down. The living room is adjacent to the bathroom where I packed away the roll of carpet. Now an angry swarm of yellow and orange, louder than the diesel engine of an 18-wheeler, is painting the ceiling of the entire first floor. Then the flashover happens all at once, bounding fire around the walls.

Sergeant Briggs is laying on his side with what looks like a beam or two on top of him. The ceiling structure must have fallen after being weakened by the fire. The fire that I created.

He's not moving.

He's barely breathing as his midsection isn't taking in deep breaths.

The sergeant's leg is bent to the side, unnaturally. It looks like he fell or was knocked down by the fallen beams.

His 6.8 liter cylinder of oxygen only supplies him with roughly 35 minutes of breathing air. It's been about 30 minutes.

I considered the contentment I might feel by watching this family man drown under the smoke before me and die with his pulse in my hand, but there's really only one way to know for sure.

I walk over to him and detach the Velcro strap holding the tank strapped around his waist. The red ring attaching the breathing tube into his breathing mask is twisted counterclockwise, and pulled apart. I pull on the backpack behind him causing the shoulder straps to easily slide off his arms. The tank is thrown far away from him across the room. Its heavy and useless like him at this point.

By grabbing his collar with my left hand I yank him away from the front door. To the opposite side from where the dark smoke is originating. Straight through the backdoor. I leave his lifeless body in the dirt behind the house.

Right as I look up after dropping off my load, the two firemen run up. In the distance, I can see a family of four on their hands and knees coughing up their lungs.

One of them speaks out of breath, "The house next door is clear."

"What the fuck happened to Sergeant Briggs!" He realizes his leader is on the ground behind me.

The youngest races over and immediately takes account of the Sergeant. He begins chest compressions after timing a slow pulse on his watch.

I stand there as motionless as their leader. Watching him be revived back into the real world.

The other teammate asks, "what the fuck happened in there, man?"

I stare into his adrenaline soaked eyes with dilated pupils. I have no response for him. Anything I say will be relayed to our superiors.

What a magnificent sight.

I feel no pain or remorse for what they're going through. Instead, a sense of pride.

That's a brand-spanking new feelin', ain't it boy.

I’m pleased that I was able to present this team with an opportunity to validate themselves. To earn a day’s work and to save their superior. They’ll go satisfied that they live to fight fire another day.

I’ll return to my box content that I can remove life as simply as I can give birth to flame.

My hands can induce a chain reaction of chemical events, and involve people like elements in a science experiment.

This town, and its citizens, are my material to do with as I please.

To move around like chess pieces, and off them one by one, or return them to the board whenever I see fit.

A subtle touch, with gentle care, to repair the tears of my body.
Unaware of their own damage, their sole discreet maladies

Chapter 6

Every Second Counts

The moment I arrived home I crashed on my bed. After removing the jacket and throwing the blood drenched gloves in a black trash bag, I collapsed on my empty mattress. Without concern for the soot and dried blood that would smear.

It could have been the excitement. It may have been the significant loss of blood.

But laying in a cold pond of my own blood awoke me in a cold chill several hours later. I don't have an air conditioner, and being low in iron is likely the cause of my current shakes.

Now that I'm up and walking around in a daze, the sweater wrapped around my incision is blotching red patches of blood on everything it touches. My hand-me-down home is a scene out of Carrie.

I walk outside, onto the gravel driveway where my shitbox is parked, overcast by perpetual clouds. To the trunk where a first aid kit is placed next to my duffel bag of torture items.

I quickly bring it back inside to ensure none of my nosy neighbors can see my arm dripping on the white rocks.

Inside the kit is a suture pack with a curved needle, forceps, and nylon thread. First thing is first, I need to wash out whatever the fuck went in when I sliced my arm open.

I'm in my narrow bathroom in the tight stand up shower where there's a light right above my head. After removing the sweater wrapped around my arm and also throwing it into the black trash bag I dragged in, I turn the showerhead to cold. It's always cold, the water heater has been broken for years.

Like a sponge being squeezed, my body is rinsed of red paint cascading onto the lemon color floor of the fiberglass shower. I raise my arm and center the open folds of the gash to the shower holes pushing out a light pressure of ice water.

It stings but not how one would expect. It's a strange sensation, cold exogenous fluid entering the subcutaneous opening at body temperature. I don't use soap, I just rub inside the lining of my forearm gently with the tips of my fingers, to not cause any more damage.

My towel, which I remembered to wash several months back, is patted against the laceration. It will be harder to stitch tissue that is beaded with water. I rinse the cut with hydrogen peroxide and enjoyably watch the foam build before me. I let it air dry.

Sitting on my toilet, without a seat cover, to let the blood drain into the bowl, I feel around the sides of my forearm hoping I don't find any shards of glass underneath. My concern is shed as I don't feel anything but loose skin.

I learned emergency medical service during my fire training. There are basic techniques that will go a long way in a contingency.

Slowly with attention to detail I begin piercing the skin closest to me with the needle being held by the forceps and nylon tied through the hold at the end.

The first puncture enters smoothly and the thread is pulled all the way until the knot I tied at the other end of the string is almost fixed against it.

The second piercing takes multiple tries as my skin is damaged and couldn't remain in place sufficiently to be poked. But with my middle and pinky finger I pinch it so to make it easier for the needle to be jabbed through. I tie a square knot twice and close the skin tight.

The third hole, 5 millimeters apart from the first two, gives me trouble. The thin layer of fat and accumulating blood under my skin is making everything lubricous. I keep having to wipe down the wound with my bath towel. I try to re-poke the hole multiple times, and after the 5th attempt I've made a gash branch out into a separate cut. It's almost as if there's something under my skin preventing the needle from penetrating the epidermis.

It appears you've left debris inside your arm, ol' chap.

I feel around the inside of the gash, almost under my skin, with my middle finger. I'm now unsure if there really is a small piece of glass I missed that is pushing up not allowing for a clean stitch.

She speaks: *My dear if you stitch it with contaminated things inside, you'll get an infection.*

You'll lose an arm at the cost of not bein' patient! The farmer is right.

With tweezers I found also inside the first aid kit, I begin digging around. Painstakingly slow and methodically, I begin digging into the bloody groove to search for a buried see-through object. Every few centimeters, I stab the layer under the fat and twist the end of the tweezers around inside me. Pulling and yanking at my flesh, taking small chunks of meat with every probe. I'm having to wipe away the tissue sticking between the end of tweezers on the towel.

This is futile. There's blood coating the bathroom floor, and soon to overflow the toilet in crimson juice. I've splashed blood along the walls in my frustration after slamming the injured arm against the sink. The needle and thread feels lubricated at this point, and the forceps to hold it are now glazed with my red epidermal fat.

#

Against any judgment I walk myself to the closest emergency room. My paranoia tells me not to drive my vehicle as to leave no record of me being at the fire.

Best to leave the vehicle at home, there boyo.

Ya' don't want to leave yer mark with that rust bucket.

I don't have any form of insurance and I'm using the license given to me after passing driver's ed during my senior year. Even though, my face looks different now.

The inside of a hospital is confusing to me. It looks disorganized with different sorts of people. All types of humans are spread out in the waiting room, and staff with different uniforms are all walking around. Different colored lines on the shiny floor lead into different directions.

My name gets called an hour or two after waiting in a small chair. At this point, I'm sure the inflammation in my arm has reached maximum capacity because I can loudly feel my pulse throbbing, and blood clotting has begun to scaffold within it. This is going to be an irritating process.

Don't you go get yer panties in a twist while yer here.

A small nurse calls my name from a room labeled TRIAGE. I don't expect to answer any prying questions, but I prepare myself mentally to stay quiet.

"Mr. Strickland." She stares right at my direction, "come on back, honey".

She stands at the entrance of the door and watches me walk into her strange room.

The deep voice of reason, *There's no need to incriminate yourself now is there?*

Her name tag says Lizbeth. Did she request her name to be shortened on a professional identifier, or is she so trashy like me with an unorthodox name given to her?

She glances at my arm wrapped three different ways in gauze, with a juicy red mark going down the middle.

She begins unwrapping my arm which causes me to take a deep breath. Not because of pain but out of surprise that she would start pulling apart my bandages like she knows me.

"Looks like a wicked scratch you've got there."

She must be stupid. How did she land this job.

She takes my vitals and asks in almost an endearing voice, "Is it ok if I lift your finger, I just need to get your pulse?".

I nod.

She places the pulse oximeter on my middle finger, with blood still encrusted underneath my nail beds.

"So, what did you do to yourself?"

How the fuck does she know that I did this?

“It was an accident.”

“We get people that try to suture themselves all the time. It’s smart that you came in.”

Careful, chap.

I don’t say a word. I know that she is required to report anything that may seem like a criminal act was committed.

She takes a closer look at the wound, and types something away in her computer. And then abruptly gets up.

“Come on, let’s get you back to stitch this up.” She smiles at me while holding the door open.

Walking ahead of me she situates me in a small exam room. I sit on the paper bed like a child dangling his legs. Lizbeth steps out.

“I’ll be right back, sugar.”

#

She comes back into the room she walked me into, with supplies in tow. What looks like antiseptic liquid, a larger suture kit, and different kinds of bandages inside sanitized plastic material.

She sits down next to me and waits with me for the attending doctor to arrive.

“So do you live close by?”

“I do.”

"You did the first suture really well, I can tell you tied a square knot. Where did you learn that?" She grabs my arm and turns it for a better view again without asking.

"I'm a volunteer fireman."

Yer as dumb as a bag of hammers!

The female voice revolts: *Why are you telling her your secrets?*

Lizbeth smiles immediately and looks at me. She's inches from my face.

Both of her arms are covered in tattoos. Her ass is large enough to notice inside her scrub pants. She's not wearing a wedding ring, and her nails are plain and short.

"That is so cool! You must have a lot of wild stories."

"No."

"Oh, ok." She keeps grinning with a twinkle in her eyes.

Just as I was going to respond that I am new to the job, the doctor walks in loudly and begins asking me abrupt questions and ordering her around.

"Nurse, turn on the procedure light."

"Yes, sir." She snaps out of her seat.

"Hello young man. My name is Dr. Anas and it looks like you've got a pretty good cut, is that right?"

"Yes."

He stares at me in a different way than Lizbeth. He looks at me from head to toe. I think he's trying to analyze me.

He's putting on blue latex gloves while maintaining his intense gaze. And as soon as he takes his seat he begins spreading the wound open while moving is head around to get a better view.

"So what did you do, pal!?"

"I fell."

"Looks like a little more than a fall. This is a deep incision with puncture wounds inside and out. As well as capillary bursting around the injury."

He looks over to Lizbeth, which makes her jump into action and begin typing notes on the computer.

This guy's a god damn quack!

"It looks like you've really caused additional damage to the initial laceration. Nurse, let's get iodine and gauze pads. Sir, I'm going to have to clean this out after what you did to yourself. Unfortunately this is going to be painful, so please try to stay still."

This motherfucker doesn't understand pain.

"There may be debris like glass or something inside." I preamble the procedure.

"Why would there be debris inside? Is that why you were poking at it?"

I can't afford to respond. So it's an awkward confrontation of silence while we lock eyes waiting for the other to budge. It's a long 83 seconds. I counted.

"Anyway, let's get started." He loses this game of chicken and moves out of the way first.

The entire time he's pouring and wiping the brown cleaning material on my arm, Nurse Lizbeth is glaring at me. Watching for any reaction.

I don't have any reactions. This isn't painful. This is bothersome at best.

Remember to thank them so they don't suspect you were breaking and entering. The woman's voice keeps me out of trouble with instructions that don't make sense.

"I just remembered I should thank you. I wasn't breaking into a home or anything. I was doing construction on my house."

Jesus Christ on a stick! The fucking hick yells at me.

"Mmm,kay" he doesn't even look up while saying it with inflection.

Chap, let's not give them a reason to look into you.

Nurse Lizbeth giggles at my remark.

"Son, whatever you were doing, you should be more careful next time. This could have been worse than it looks."

That shit looks like a stomped possum. His stupid country sayings.

He's right, darling. She concurs with him.

Nurse Lizbeth speaks up, "We see guys try to repair their skin all the time. Infection is way more common than you'd think".

She says it with a smile, but removes it once the doctor looks over to her.

I'm infected with more than bacteria at this point. I have the disease that riddles me discontent unless I'm hurting others.

But I just need to be more prudent about my intentions. I can't believe I didn't see the glass window before exiting. I should have done a better job with the stitching. Coming in here was a mistake.

But my ruminating thoughts, as loud as the voices, are dissolved to a halt by the clang of the iodine bottle being dropped on the metal tray. The nurse scurries to pick up the bottle and steps on a latch to throw it away in a trashcan along the exam room wall.

Ironically, he doesn't find any glass. He proceeds to suture it slowly and less rough than how I did.

There's something I can learn from him. That slow and careful will develop better results. That it's possible to repair a dire situation with meticulous work.

That a simple look can put a woman in her place.

#

I return home after being discharged. It's early in the afternoon. I change my clothes and pack my monocular in a smaller bag. As well a bird whistle in case I'm stopped by any authority. I've learned about some local birds so that I can spell out some basic birdwatching facts to excuse carrying around stalking equipment. No one likes a Peeping Tom, and I can't give any officer of the law a reason to investigate me.

I drive right back to the hospital.

I knew you were fond of that young nurse. The professor calls me out.

I find where the employees park, and back up my Civic to the adjacent parking lot.

I'm waiting for her. If there's one thing for sure, she'll appear sooner or later. Every work shift comes to an end.

#

She finally walks out.

I've been in the car for three hours. It's surprising that medical personnel get off at 7 pm. 12 hours on and 12 hours off is very different than a fireman's schedule. If I would have known this, I might have gotten a bite to eat. I would have gone home to rub one out to her Myspace image prior to following her around town.

My stomach is hurting. It's always hurting.

But Lizbeth looks tired.

She's still wearing the same scrubs she was wearing when we met inside the emergency room earlier, but with a jacket unzipped over her top.

She drives slowly out of the parking lot. I take my time to exit as well. She doesn't rush to getting to where she's going, and I shouldn't become impatient now while trailing behind.

I'm fascinated by her. Her big brown eyes and perfect eyebrows are now in my head. Her body is dancing circles for me.

I follow her across town to a shopping center with children walking around. She goes into a daycare center and comes out with a small boy.

Motherfucker. I can't do what I was planning to do.

#

Five days later and I've been following her to and from work this entire time. Over the weekend she remained mostly indoors at her apartment and then at some family member's house. I'm assuming her mother's. Several people arrived while she was staying over there. There was a woman slightly older who kind of looks like her, an older couple, and multiple children frolicking around on the yard.

It's now Tuesday.

Today her routine has changed. She's normally dragging her child around town before and after work. But today she's alone.

This morning she skipped her usual stop at the coffee shop on her way to the hospital. She also didn't pull over to the usual daycare provider in the shopping center.

She's wearing her normal scrubs and hospital issued jacket to the emergency room.

One wonders if it has to do with the vehicle that dropped by last night. The professor hypothesizes a good point.

I was forced to park quite far from her apartment building the evening prior due to all the parking spots being taken.

I did see a man get out, but my vision was occluded by a petite dog walker that almost looked like her. And we all know how much I love a bitch in leggings walking with a leash.

I figure that was her ex, wasn't it? That baby's daddy, ain'it?

No wonder she doesn't have her child, and she likely wouldn't have left the toddler at home alone. She doesn't remind me of my mother.

I'll return here to the same parking lot toward the end of her shift. I have two college courses to attend and I might be on call at the station. But I've been holding off on calling out for a sick day for a day like today.

Because today is ripe with opportunity.

Today, she's going to get it.

All of me.

State of mind on safety. Wasted on luck.
Tested during invasion. First in line to get fucked.

Chapter 7

Entering and Breaking

There she is, in view of my car's side mirror. She's closer than she appears and within my grasp.

But I can't grab hold of her here. Not yet.

This is going to take patience and some finesse.

It's 7:15 p.m. and she's walking to her car like clockwork, that looks orange under the streetlamp.

She's not rushing as she usually does. Her footsteps seem slower and despondent.

#

Only a 15 minute drive and we've pulled into her apartment complex. I'm two cars behind her, just like in the action movies.

I know she hasn't noticed me. She's pulled into her usual parking spot right in front of her apartment building. She gets out of the driver seat without looking around or even in my direction.

Watching her walk up the stairs into the hallway of her building makes me salivate. Her ass visibly bounces to the left and right. From this distance the silver jewelry around her neck is glistening and accentuating her pale neck. As she turns her body to open the door while choosing her key off the heavy lanyard, standing there under the dim light of the worn down building, her profile and tattoos on her arms are deliciously outlined.

She walks in without care or awareness that her demise is but seconds away.

I can see her kitchen light has been flicked on soon after entering her premises.

She normally begins preparing dinner for her incomplete family by now. I know this because she opens a window to let the smells out. Today she hasn't.

There's an eerie calmness inside her small home. Not much activity, absent the usual laughing and yelling that occurs between mother and child. I haven't seen her walk around, as her shadow tends to pass by the drapes while chasing her toddler around on most evenings.

I'm waiting for a sign that she hasn't fallen asleep or that she isn't taking a shower. Any sign of life in there and I'm charging in to remove it.

#

I've been waiting for what feels like an entire night. But it's only been 70 minutes.

Just as I'm considering the metal gutter lining down her building to get a view inside of her window, a shadow from a small stature walks across the kitchen.

Right on cue. She slides open the kitchen window.

There she is in front of the stove. I know because of the enticing smells emitting through her cheap screen.

Reminds me of grits with bacon.

This fucking hillbilly.

Lizbeth is waiting for you, my dearest.

She's right. There's no time like the present. And if I'm to do this I won't get another opportunity like the current one. What a waste of my talents if I don't act with purpose. Just like I learned from the Sergeant. Carefully how I watched the doctor perform.

In the trunk of my vehicle there's a fireman's helmet and jacket from when I burned down that house. I never intended to return them to the truck and they never asked during the commotion of the Sergeant's failing condition.

I put on the helmet and jacket prior to my ascent into her apartment building. I don't need a camera capturing the face of the person that is doing what I'm about to do.

#

Through the doorway is music blaring, "Wrong Side Of Heaven" – FFDP. Which is a promising sign that whatever happens in there wont be heard by ears on the outside.

No matter how loud she fights and screams, there is no one in the vicinity that can help her now.

Three loud knocks with my visor down. It has Detroit Fire Department stamped on the front in bright gold lettering.

Seconds slow down and I'm imagining what she's doing and where she is on the other side of this door. I wonder what she's wearing because I'm planning to rip everything off.

She responds soon after from the far end of her small hole in the wall.

"Who is it!?"

Time to pull the wool over her eyes, boy. The farmer sounds serious.

"Fire department! Ma'am do you have your gas stove on?!"

An emergency backed by a government issued uniform is a sure way to open any premises.

"Oh my goodness, I do! One moment!"

Here she comes lad. Be at the ready.

The professor is right. I pull out my foldable shovel and hold it down low by my side after clicking it straight.

I can hear her raising the latch and peering through the peephole.

The door is clicked unlocked.

Steady…

It creaks open and the rubber lining the bottom of her door rubs inward into her space. Making a slow swiping noise against the faux tile. Her small, tattooed hands grab the door to spread it open.

The smell of her skin and a whiff of her cooking rushes out as she swiftly opens the door.

My body and every muscle within it receives a flood of adrenaline.

Like a Sundarbans tiger, lowering his body before it pounces on its prey. Coming out of the bush to rip the body apart.

She's dead already, she just hasn't been told yet.

Word salad and nonsense herbs of wisdom
Are worthless when at the chasm of Dante's prison.

Chapter 8

Lizbeth

It's at the precise moment I see her dilated brown eyes of angst that I force the door wide and show her the shovel near her head.

I charge into her. Pushing her body deep inside. And kick the door closed behind me.

"Don't you fucking say a word!" I yell behind the helmet.

A direct command at a moment of alerted distress often results in obedience. I learned this at the fire academy.

She gasps as she backsteps, and trips over a small carpet in the living room. Catching herself on her fists.

I raise the shovel above my head as to strike down on her like a log. I swing it with force and all of my weight. And stop at the last second inches away from her delicate face.

She screeches while squeezing her eyes shut, "Eeeeh".

There it is, that's the opportunity you've been looking for.

Still carrying the serrated shovel, I overstep her small body and grab a fist of her dry hair.

To drag her into the kitchen for what I have planned.

The stove is still on and fuming a nutritious pot of food.

She's crying and squeaking her adorable voice while holding on to my hands. She kicking her muscular legs and knocks over the coffee table as she's dragged backwards on her back.

What a surprise she hasn't screamed just yet. The woman relays.

On the vinyl floor near her kitchen table she stands up immediately, jumping up, making a run for it. Like a bat out of a fucking cave. I grasp her by the cotton collar and pull her body toward me. I push her toward the boiling pot of food and push her head down with a knot of hair inside my hands. I dropped the shovel as soon as she tried to escape.

"Keep it up and I'll dunk your fucking head in." I warn.

She's still in her green scrubs. But in the tussle of securing her body I ripped her top down the back. I now begin working on her scrub pants with both hands. She falls naturally once I yank on the elastic seam, tripping her. She's kicking again and beginning to scream. Her top is pulled upward and discarded once fully ripped off.

"Get off me!!!" she twists her body left and right, swinging her legs at my arms away from her. "Oh my god! NO!! NO!!!"

Pause.

I point the shovel at her face again. The sharp point is inches away from her smooth forehead.

"You move and I'll shove this into your pretty face."

She's shaking. Her whole body is vibrating like a leaf in the wind. Not speaking, not breathing, but holding her breath. And staring at me. At the visor covering my face.

I look around her small five by five kitchen for a fixture to lock her onto. Nothing obvious in sight.

"Stand up and put your hands on the counter." I point to the small surface that appears to double as a bar.

I doubt she's ever had anyone over for a nightcap. Today she'll finally get to use the bar, to serve me with her fluids.

But she doesn't move a muscle. She's frozen in fear.

She's still wearing her bra and in a two-birds-one-stone approach, I attempt to lift her by using the front of her bra as a handle. Obviously it snaps right off before her torso is lifted into the space above her.

The song just ended, and a new one has begun, "Enter Sandman" – Metallica.

"AHHhhhh!" she exclaims when the elastic bra is removed.

She instantly covers her breasts and bright pink nipples hardened by panic.

So to assist her, I grab her by the neck with both hands and stand her up. She must weigh about 115 lbs. Less than a firehose.

Standing on her toes, I can smell her breath seeping under my visor. It smells like a woman's breath. Fresh and subtle.

Maybe out of anger, more likely out of excitement, I throw her small upper body over onto the counter. She's slammed on her stomach and her knees crash against the cabinets underneath.

"Uuhng" she lets out a fraction of air from her diaphragm.

Her eyes are closed. She doesn't seem to be fully aware of what's about to happen. Her hands are over her head rubbing the pain out her scalp after being pulled on.

To my left is a kitchen towel. Approximately 28 inches in length. Sufficient to tie her wrists tight.

In her stillness I take advantage of her amenable limbs and turn her arms around to her back. She barely tenses and doesn't put up much of a fight.

"Please don't do this. PLEASE." She begs to turn me on.

You're certainly required to do this, chap.

A simple double-knot binds her two wrists tight.

I shove her against the counter again and push her arms up toward her neck. Coming close to ripping her shoulders and causing significant pain.

"Fuck! Fuck! Fuck!" She's starting to freak out.

With my other hand I push up my visor all the way through. The helmet falls off behind me and the clattering noise makes her already shivering body jolt.

Slowly, the same hand begins tugging on the seam of her scrub bottoms past her knees and down to her ankles. She's still wearing her sneakers, and combined with the pants it makes for a useful restraint of her two thick legs.

"Oh my god, oh my god, oh my.." she's panicking.

Shut her trap up.

To our left is a large bottle of olive oil she used moments earlier to cook herself food. The top is still serendipitously uncapped. Without thinking twice, I pour the contents of the oil all over her. From her head, down to her back, and on her vanilla hams. It's streaming down her thick legs and pooling into her socks.

She gasps and then closes her breathing tube as the cold temperature hits her supple skin, "Hhhuggh."

I pull out of my pocket the only lighter I own and hold it close to her face, to ensure she can see it in my grip. The wheel is pulled and a small flame is held close to her dripping face. It's waved against her arm skin, close enough so that she can feel it's heat. Olive oil is combustible yet not flammable, but she sure as fuck doesn't know that. She looks down at her chest and the rest of her body to make sense of what is currently happening.

She looks back in an attempt to look at me and something about her oily posture, bent over with her back arched, makes me instantly hardened. I snap the lighter on over and over again to scare her straight. She immediately starts urinating, all over her floor. Which somehow makes her even sexier.

A fist of her now wet hair is gripped yet again, with my five fingers pulling her hair back, and causing her neck to bend back 90 degrees. She's crying.

"Wha wha why are you doing this? Who whoo are you?" she bellows out.

I wonder if some tv show taught her to maintain conversation with her assailant. She won't get any communication from me. Instead she gets her face slammed against the cold countertop.

A thumb all the way in her ass makes it official that she's going to be violated. Immediately her body reacts and begins jerking around like a woman being raped in her kitchen.

I let go of her hair and pop out the entirety of my thumb from inside to walk over to her fridge. I quickly peer inside, but in the corner of my eye I see her moving around already. Looking around, looking for me.

A large cucumber is sitting on the shelf next to the milk. It’s too obvious.

Returning to my victim, I punch her right in the ribs. Just between her floating rib and true ribs. Enough to make her suck in a pound of air and lock up her diaphragm.

“HHUUHG.”

My hand is over her neck holding her face down against the bar.

The cucumber is thick and my middle finger and thumb barely meet around on one end. In her vagina it goes.

“Jesus fucking Christ! OWW! Stop! No!! NO!!!!” she finally begins to scream.

I don’t insert it slowly, because it requires a forceful push to get past her long inner vaginal lips. A thick vagina that I can visibly see from the back as it protrudes out within both closed legs.

About a quarter of the vegetable is inside her and she’s standing herself taller on the tips of her toes. I’m shoving it inside her in an upwards direction to make her asshole stick out a little more.

I want to make her really cry.

The cucumber is inserted right up to my knuckles. More than half, about 75% of it is inside her.

“UUUHHhhhh! Oh my fucking god!!!” She whines past her gripped teeth.

It’s being inserted all the way in and almost all the way out, now in a slightly downward direction. Making her stand on the flats of her feet while her arms are being bent back in an unnatural position. Faster. And then even faster. Parts of my knuckles are even going inside her as I can feel her smaller lips rub against the back of my hands.

"OW! OW! OW!" With each thrust of the foot long cucumber. She's sobbing in between breaths.

Just as I'm having a thought that the cucumber is resistant to being bent at this angle, that the front wall of her vagina is putting it to the test, it cracks in half.

"AAAAHHHH!!! AAAAAGGHHHHH!!!" she cries out.

Now that is a succulent scream. The woman's voice inside my head describes.

The half inside her disappears behind her pink flesh and the other is left in my hand. What a pretty surprise.

She's squirming around in agony, to what appears like a genuine response to pain.

My dick is dripping and pulsating underneath my jeans. I can't keep it tucked away any longer. So after I unzip and pull my pants down, I slowly force it into her uniquely shaped anus. It's a skin colored mound that resembles the knot at the end of a balloon. The cucumber broken inside her vaginal cavity is pushing back and making it a real task to get myself inside her body.

Half of my dick is inside her and it feels as if the muscle surrounding her rectum is gripping my shaft. Like a thick slimy rubberband making it strenuous but so god damned pleasurable to squeeze myself past into her backside.

She squeals once more with her face shoved into the cold counter, "AAAAGGGGHH!!! Ma Ma Mammeeee!!!!"

I start getting a rhythm going. Piercing her shiny flesh with my hardened member. I can feel the edge of the cucumber from inside her asshole. It's rubbing against the bottom of my dick every time I insert it. Her back is dripping in a mixture of cooking oil and sweat. Her head is lifted into the air and every muscle is tightened.

"Ungh, Ungh, Ungh" she grunts with every thrust going deep inside. "I! I! I! Please Stop!".

She needs to be punished. For being who she is.

While inside her, while holding her arms tight, my other hand is rummaging through the drawers to my left.

Near the stove, each drawer contains different utensils she uses to cook food for herself and her child. A wooden spoon is taken out to be the perfect whipping tool.

"Are you a piece of meat?" I gently ask her while slowing down my thrusts. Still rhythmically pushing her shit in and pulling the knot out for me to see.

No answer.

"I said! Are you a fucking piece of meat!?"

She screams bloody murder, "AAAHHHHH!!!"

That there is not a valid answer. The hick is right.

I whip her lower back. Right between the two dimples connecting her buttocks to her torso, three times with the wooden spoon. Immediately causing red welts.

"Are. You. A. Piece. Of. Fucking. Meat!?" I repeat myself while emphasizing each word with seven thrusts into her ass.

Still no god forsaken answer.

She's obviously not aware of your question. The deep voice contests.

She needs to be made aware.

Three more whips with the wooden spoon. Again on the lower end of her back. This time I'm aiming for her dimples with the first two hits, and the third smacks her perfectly right in the middle over her spine.

"LIZBETH!" I call out her name during a pause while I'm fully inside her.

Her head immediately raises and she attempts aggressively to look behind at me.

"Wha, wha.. How the fu...?" There's a question of terror in her voice.

I whip the back of her head with the wooden spoon. And it breaks in half to fly across the room.

She screeches. "EEEHHhh! HHELLLLLPPP!!!!!"

I find a great cadence now with four thrusts into her tight asshole, "Are You! A Fucking!! Piece Of!!! Meat???"

"YES! YES! YES!!!"

She finally responds before I even finish the last push into her greasy body.

Without hesitation, the blender near her head is detached from the wall and I take the cord into my hand. Like a lasso it's wrapped around her neck. I'm pulling it away from her to tighten the loop around her throat. Making her carotid arteries bulge out even more.

Make her say it. She says in my head.

"Answer the fucking question!" I keep my voice raised while out of breath from all the ass fucking. "ARE YOU A PIECE OF MEAT!"

My dick is all the way inside her rectum. Her arms are still tied and unnaturally close to her upper back. And through her constricted breathing tube from the plastic cable wrapped around her small neck she whispers in a barely audible phrase.

"I'm a piece of meat." She's able to choke out.

Right then and there I ejaculate. With one grasp on her bound wrists and the other holding her makeshift leash, she's pounded into the structure inside the safety of her home. The plastic cord is raised high into the air making her face visibly purple. And as soon as I burst my semen into her rectum, against the broken cucumber lodged inside her vaginal canal, she begins shaking violently.

She's bloody convulsing.

And to my chagrin I let go of her oiled limbs and release the cord from my fingers. She's jerking her body uncontrollably, right out of my grip. The slickness of her skin makes her hard to hold down.

The olive oil has sponged into her sneakers and it has leaked past her scrub pants to puddle under the rubber of her soles. She collapses to the side after slipping her weight off the counter over the laminated floors.

And with her goes the heavy blender still attached to her neck. Because her hands are behind her, her head whips into the hard floor after her shoulder is the first to hit the floor. The metal appliance crushes into the back of her head after her skull dribbles off the kitchen floor. Creating a crunching sound from her wet face.

She's not moving anymore. She's bleeding everywhere and a small river is starting to form.

Her head is flat on its right side, with her right shoulder on the ground, and the left side of her body in the air. Lizbeth is twisted and toneless, mangled by the fall and ensuing heavy blender. Her wet hair is muddled on the hard floor with a thick swirl of sweat, oil, and blood.

I tuck away my soiled cock and step over her lifeless body.

I don't have my tools and I don't consider doing anything else.

I'm still out of breath and semen is still leaking out all over her.

I'm taking a mental picture of the position of her body and the curves that have been oiled.

She's done. She got what she deserved.

But there's no need to disturb the dead.

I can see my way out.

To relive the moral injury. To revisit the cemetery.
To remission, in due time, back to recidivism.

Chapter 9

Insubordination

It's been an entire 24 hours. Nighttime again.

And I'm still high on adrenaline. I haven't stopped sweating. My breaths are at about 25 inhales per minute, I can't slow them down. I can only count as they inflate my chest and expel out of my control.

I found my way back to this plastic home. And I'm pacing up and down the tight hallway leading into my smaller room. There's no way I can sleep. Reclining on my back is inconceivable.

I can't sit down. I can't pause my mind for even a moment.

Masturbating is not an option at the present time. My member is not responding and strangely remains in its flaccid state.

Her smell, her taste, is still lodged within my nasal cavities. And I don't want to shower to rid myself of her fluids. My hands are coated with the grease I poured all over her, mixed with whatever delicious lotion she was wearing. My dick is still encrusted with the juices from inside her asshole. A layer of white with red streaks is painted on my shaft, presumably from the tearing of her sphincter. Even drops of her brain matter are still splattered onto my knees from when her head was bashed open.

You seem to have had fun last night didn't you, my dear? Mrs. Bathory asks.

Last night, I lost… control. That wasn't supposed to happen. I'm in deep, deep trouble.

"I killed a woman. I just put myself away." I repeat aloud. "Just put myself away".

Don't ya have a hissy fit now, ya got what ya wanted. Farmer John clarifies the obvious for me.

My thoughts are racing ahead of me.

Honestly ol' boy, your execution was spot on. Professor Marks provides some much needed feedback.

"But I killed a woman I just met. And left my DNA like some fucking rookie!"

No use crying over split milf, now is there? John has a point.

"I'm not crying over her life." I throw a small radio across the home.

"I'm freaking out about being caught on camera. Not just as the hospital, but at the entrance of her complex!"

My pacing is getting faster. The trailer home is swaying as I traverse from one end to the other.

I haven't eaten anything in about 48 hours. My stomach is almost as loud as the voices. But one loses their appetite after getting a taste of womanslaughter.

You should get some sustenance, sweetheart. She's not wrong.

Seems like you're doubting the results of your work. Mr. Solomon's profound voice offers deep thought.

"My semen is going to be filed in some database, and I'll be eventually found!"

First of all, you're giving the Detroit police excessive credit, my dear. Secondly, the olive oil you used was enough to taint any collection. Mrs. Bathory attempts to defuse my concerns.

"I can't believe you all pushed me to do this." I complain.

Now look who's regrettin' his own doggone decisions!

Are you a retard, ol' chap?

"Fuck you! I'm not stupid! This is my life you're fucking with!"

I throw the hotplate across the room. It slams against the wall, shattering the panel off of it. No chance of getting a warm meal now.

Then quit being spineless, and act like a man. She scolds me right as the appliance lands.

"I'm not being weak. I'm trying to be smart!" I contest to no avail.

I catch a glimpse of my reflection against the hazy mirror inside the bathroom. I don't recognize the man in the mirror. He's not what I want.

Somehow my arm is bleeding again. I'm using the same dirty towel with previous stains to wipe the goop leaking out of my bandages. I'm unsure if I ripped them during the attack or just now.

Ya keep this up and you'll rip them stitches like a hog caught on a wire.

There isn't any feeling in my entire external body. I'm numb to pain, but I feel every pinch of my internal conflict.

It could be your performance that's giving you second thoughts. The baritone pipes something hurtful.

"What, what do you mean?" I'm stumped.

Maybe you didn't last as long as you wanted, dearest. Mrs. Bathory has some nerve.

Ya know what, the moment he choked her he couldn't hold his load! The redneck is taunting me, laughing.

Look mate, we all have our peculiarities. You just need to work on your stamina. The Englishman is passive aggressive.

"I wasn't aware that I needed to last longer during a fucking rape."

Now I'm getting heated. If I thought I was sweating earlier, now I'm saturated in saltwater dripping off my chin.

A hole in the bathroom wall by way of my fist seems fitting. If I could, I'd also murder the personalities in my mind. To erase their presence and the memories that come with them.

More importantly, you should've sliced her throat to prevent her from screaming, my precious. Her hindsight is not helpful right now.

You didn't even use your bag of tricks. Professor Marks criticizes.

What if her screams caught the attention of a neighbor who saw you leave? Mr. Solomon plants a seed.

Did ya even wear the mask on yer way out, ya nitwit?

"Fuck! I left my lighter!" I exclaim out of pure shock that I could make such a mistake.

Jesus Christ on a stick, your criminal signature!

Oh my heavens, your fingerprints!

You fucking idiot!

I'm in the kitchen with a steak knife in hand. Shaking, not only my head left and right, but my hands are trembling.

I'm not steady. I'm not stable.

There's a high probability that I'm going to do life in a prison cell for taking her worthless life.

This was all for nothing.

#

I'm back in the vehicle that my mother left me when she left for good. But I don't know how I got here. I don't remember going outside or getting in without anyone looking at me.

I don't have a destination. I'm allowing the voices to take the wheel.

The speedometer is on a low number. I'm trying to be excessively careful to not make any moving violations. I have an eerily feeling that I'm the person of interest, that I'm being looked for.

Ya need to see if her place is littered with the boys in blue. If they is, then you're fried as a fish.

I pull into her apartment complex which seems like a huge error in judgment.

"I shouldn't be here. This is suicide."

One is best informed when seeing it with your own eyes. Solomon's dark voice vibrates inside me.

"But I can't go anywhere near her building. What if a neighbor..."

And just as I was going to finish my thought, I pull up on a gaggle of law enforcement vehicles surrounding the place. Blue coats are scattered about, walking, talking, and probing at the crime scene.

Just as we expected. Mrs. Bathory states the obvious.

It's quite safe to assume they haven't looked into her arse just yet, have they my boy? Professor Marks makes a funny.

I bet they're running this dummy's lighter for DNA. Farmer John is a pseudo attorney now.

"I can't be here. We should go." I U-turn around hoping I'm not spotted.

A loud bang claps into the air. What sounds like a gunshot.

The backfire of my car garners some of the officer's attention. Multiple sets of eyes are in my direction. I'm being watched as I signal that I'm making a right turn, and accidentally run over the curb. Causing more screeching sounds. Making more officers notice me.

This boy is as dumb as a rock!

Steady, mate!

My head is pointed straight ahead, but eyes are darting around. Expecting to be pulled over in a heartbeat.

#

I'm on the same route that I've travelled multiple times while stalking her. And like a flashback of some horrific trauma, I'm transported back at the scene.

I'm right there in the moment. The moment when I had that feeling.

The feeling that my penis felt right as I was ejaculating. Emptying my gonads the moment she slipped and fell. Re-experiencing the sensation when the rubberband of her anus pulled my skin down from the base, past the shaft, and over the ridge of my dickhead. Like a lubricated vacuum seal making a pop when pulled apart.

It's embedded in my core memories now. The strange impression that her genitals made on my body, the very split second before she lost her life, is mouthwatering. My dick is rock hard in the driver seat. I'm squeezing the tip as hard as I can. Attempting to induce precum so I can rub it around. I taste it, in hopes that I can still taste her, but I can't.

Now you're hard, but you couldn't stand at attention before?! Mrs. Bathory attempts to embarrass me.

The daycare is on my left. Children are not walking around as they usually do. There's two black colored vehicles parked at the entrance. They're likely additional detectives looking into the crime.

One wonders if the shopping center has cameras that watched you watching her. Solomon's dark voice reverbs a legitimate concern.

There's no need to pull into the shopping center. I just drive by, toward the hospital.

#

I'm parked as I was before. In the same parking spot where I can watch the employee entrance from a reasonable distance. I haven't seen a police vehicle anywhere around, and the mysterious black cars aren't parked here yet. I expected there to be more commotion, but it's abnormally quiet for an emergency room.

Y'all remember when he couldn't get her to say she was a piece of meat?! Farmer John randomly starts riling them up.

My dear, you need to be more assertive with your victims.

"I whipped her over and over. I was trying." I contest.

Honestly fellow, confidence is bred with action. Professor Marks spells some bullshit.

I'm trying to focus on reinvigorating my erection. But their voices are distracting my thoughts from reminiscing about her.

"Just shut up for a second." I whisper while tugging on the end of my dick to wake it up.

And my focus shifts to the view in front of the windshield. Blue and red lights. Multiple cars are now filing at the employee entrance. A caravan of police officers all exit their vehicles almost in synchrony.

They're there to ask questions. To take notes and collect data. The likelihood that they're going to ask for the CCTV footage is beyond likely. My face, my medical record, even bandages used on me will be viewed at some point in time.

And as I look back down to cram my dick and balls back into my jeans, I'm surprised for the second time today that it's harder than I thought. I'm fully erect and already dripping precum down to the base of my shaft. I'm potently turned on.

The thought, the visualization that most of those men of the law have looked at my work is arousing. They have taken pictures of her mangled body, written down a description of what they think I did to her, and conferred about my reasoning for this heinous crime. I think I even saw a female cop or two, and I question if they considered what if this happened to them. These new realities of the cause and effect of my doing is an immense stimulation.

I spit on myself. As best as I can to release a sufficient amount of saliva over the hole at the end of my dick. There's not much because I haven't had water or pop for days. I'm rubbing one out at her place of work in memory of her. Watching the entrance closely while I envision what we did together.

How I desecrated her temple.

There was an instant while I pounded her backside after breaking the cucumber inside her vagina that she felt incredibly tight. I'm trying my best to recreate that clip while I use both hands to stroke myself up and down.

I'm remembering when she tried to not let me inside her asshole. I was already inside her, only past the head of my penis but trying to stuff the rest in. And Lizbeth knew that. She was already sobbing hysterically and laying on the kitchen counter stiff as a board. And she tightened her asshole, but only for a bit. She squeezed it shut with what felt like every muscle she had. That feeling is indescribable. The physicality of having to fight past her reluctance to allow me from doing what I want to do. It made me feel…powerful, that it was the stiffness of my cock against the skintight retraction of her genitals. And I won. I squeezed every inch of me within her wet rectum.

You didn't necessarily win, my dear. She gave up.

I block out Bathory's voice to focus on my fantasy.

It don't count if the whore enjoyed it!

Farmer John won't distract me from enjoying this.

Do you truly believe this was a success, ol' chap?

If it was a failure then at least I'll cum one more time with my freedom.

My eyelids close shut, rolling my eyeballs to the back of my head. I take a deep breath in and appreciate the squirt of ejaculate run over both of my hands. The thick liquid is pouring past my eight knuckles. It’s steaming warm. And providing me more lubrication to rub both hands in opposite directions making more come out.

A shining white light is glared over my face to prevent me from opening my eyes. It’s burning and makes me look away.

I try to let go. I try to get back my sight.

To the present moment.

The night's magic seems to whisper and hush.
Lullaby my baby, sleep until daddy is done.
But run if you hear a scream, this is not a dream.

Chapter 10

The Moondance Kid

Cold drops of water are trickling on the back of my neck. Both shoulders are being pounded on by heavy rainwater. My hands are numb. And I can feel my skin tighten from the horripilation effects that the thunderstorm is having on my skin.

I'm floating. My feet are moving, left and right. My body is being propelled forward because I can feel the wind cooling down my nose. But I don't know if gravity and I are conjoined. There's no pressure being formed under the soles of my feet.

The scene is a blur as my body is obviously moving through space and time. Yet, the scene before me is as detailed as a photograph being held in front of me.

I can experience my environment to its fullest, but it feels like I'm in an alternate reality. Nothing seems real and the material of this world appears less tangible now more than ever. This disconnect to the physical world around me is heightening my own realization, a deeper awareness of my self.

Everything inside me is pushing me forward to explore. Not only to go to places that I haven't been, but to corners of my mind that have yet to be uncovered.

I can't tell if my thoughts are racing or if they are just simply more coherent. As I'm imagining a life where I can do exactly just as I please.

I am god, such that I can give life to fire and take life with ease. I feel no remorse about what I've done, and I want to experience that power more.

I visualize a way of living where I am capable of accomplishing very specific goals, while carrying out the worst crimes my imagination can conjure up. I want to achieve the unachievable, but in conjunction to causing pain like no one else.

The voices that are usually echoing inside my mind are muted. They haven't left me, I can sense their presence and their watchful eyes. But I can't hear their sounds anymore. Their insults and commands are absent and no longer pushing me around.

Yet, there's a humming white noise vibrating my auditory cortex. I looked into the mechanics of hearing when The Board first appeared. I thought it strange that I can hear them when no one else could. Especially when they would curse out Mother in front of her, without eliciting any violent response. Although she usually did at the slightest provocation, since I was very young.

The world around me never seemed to be aware of them, like when they yelled at me to attack a fellow student in the locker room when it was just us. A boy who bragged moments earlier about losing his virginity to some popular girl.

He never saw me coming and acted shocked when I walked up to him without a sound out of nowhere. He didn't expect me to stuff his own sock inside his mouth even though The Board was screaming for me to do it. He stupidly opened his mouth wide in anger after I pushed him down to choke him out.

But now, there isn't a voice or anyone in control of me. I am finally free and doing as I please.

Walking without a care in the world through a neighborhood I don't recognize. In the rain. Wet from head to toe.

#

I'm striding, practically gliding down this gravel road I've ended upon, past trailer after trailer home. They all look the same with minor differences in the manner in which they decorate themselves. But monotonous and repeating at best. White and plastic with small ornaments. A wind chime or gnome to set them apart.

I'm attempting to hold onto a thought, but they're all so distant and racing past. I'm not able to grasp onto an action, no less an adverb, to describe what I want to do.

And in the most confusing moment, right to where I begin to slow down my pace to gather my thoughts, I notice a bright light to my right. Burning loud and fast like a fuse.

It's not an incandescent light, but a blaze of fire emitting a bright radiance of yellow. It's setting alight to a house and the yard in front of it. The roof is raging just like the ones I've done before. But this is different. It feels different.

No where in my repertoire of vocabulary do I have a word to describe the sensation inside me.

I'm experiencing… concern.

I can hear screaming. What sounds like an entire family. Yelling for help through the small windows beginning to crack under the heat. The home is hissing and sizzling while their bodies are trapped behind locked doors.

I do the obvious, and race over to remove them from their roasting tinder box. I have a belief that I contain the skills needed for this very situation. Not called upon by the city or to assist an engine from a neighboring station. But me, only myself is needed to save this family, and I am at the right place and right time for once.

I try to push up the closed window where the raging fire sits behind. But I pull my hands right away as they're burned and left steaming from the glass being baked inside.

I see a hose is hung on a reel right at the front corner of the trailer house. Holding onto the nozzle at the end I run away from the house to unravel it from its apparatus.

Once it's detangled and stretched to its fullest extent I run back with nozzle still in hand. I turn the knob counterclockwise to open the valve and allow maximum water to run through. And within seconds I'm spraying the house down with a piercing stream from the water hose.

I'm aiming the jet of cooling liquid to the base of the flames. That's the quickest way to smother the source of the fire.

The howls from the parents and the shrieks from the children are getting louder. It seems that the sweating fever of the burning home is closing in on them. Any moment now and the tin roof is likely to collapse over them. Time is a factor and the essence of saving their lives is to prevent their flesh from cooking. A third degree burn is a real fucking problem.

This isn't working. The light is getting brighter and the fire is expanding in size. It's time to rush in and find the children inside.

Before I know it, I'm in front of their door and staring at the handle to formulate the quickest way to break open the barrier to the inner side.

A front kick, right to the left of the knob, almost suffices to crack apart the latch from the faceplate holding it firm. The door panel has a visible crack and smoke begins to escape. The screams are roaring and impossible to ignore.

"Help!!!" "Please somebody!!!" "We're locked inside!!!"

Their pleas for help invigorate my body's resolve to give it one more kick to ensure I break open the lock holding me back.

And as expected, a stomp with my other foot is enough to swing open the cheap entrance to their plastic home. Immediately a wave of hot glow slams against my face. Halting my rush inward and pausing my step.

As I'm opening my eyes, covering my face to protect my eyelashes from searing, a force hits me in my stomach. Enough to break my posture and throw me back.

My body is lifted into the air and I'm launched backwards. I watch as the deck is distancing from my position. I've landed on the hard pavement leading into the home. My body is slammed on the concrete but I don't feel anything.

Initially I perceived it to be an explosion, maybe the consequence of oxygen diffusing into a meth lab, but that is not what this is. Because immediately, my head is being pounded upon. Over and over, a fist is slamming into my skull. Making the back of my head dribble on the hard surface beneath me.

I can't hear anything, neither fire nor crying.

All I'm experiencing is a weight on my chest and a hammer bobbing my face around out of my control.

Two hands are now around my throat. Choking the air inside me. I can't breathe. I can't remove the strangle with which I'm held.

And as my eyes are losing light and the already opaque view in front of me begins to dim, flashes of blue and red are circling around me.

There's no more heat. There's no more blazing inferno. But several tall, dark bodies surrounding me, and the ability to breathe comes back once more.

And before I can make sense of the imagery before me, to piece together the sequence of events that put me on my back, I lose consciousness.

I disappear into the night, into dreamless sleep, away from harming anyone.

Far away from being hurt.

To console thy broken life
With art, with stars, begets hope. Forgets strife.

Chapter 11

Flying Over The Cuckoo's Nest

Slowly, my eyes unfold. The surface beneath me is hard and thin. I'm cold.

Lights are bright. My head is ringing. I can feel everything now, yet my body is heavy. I can't find the needed strength to lift my arms or legs.

My face feels swollen and my eyelids are thick. Every time I blink it to open them wider, I can't.

I can perceive my body is laid flat in a horizontal position. I can raise my head and look around the room in which I've been placed. But I don't remember coming in here. I don't know where I'm at, because I've sure as hell have never been in this room before.

You really screwed the proverbial pooch, chap.

You don't need to be a university professor to uncover that fact, asshole. But I'm strangely pleased to hear a familiar voice, albeit with a funny British accent.

In walks a heavy set woman. With syringe in hand, squirting out a drop or two of strange looking medicine onto the floor.

"Hello young man, please stay calm. You're at Eloise Psychiatric Hospital. You were admitted early this morning."

"Where the fuck is Eloise hospital?"

"Detroit." She has that face of disdain like I'm supposed to be thankful for waking up to a stranger, in an unfamiliar place.

"You don't say. Why the fuck am I here?"

"You were found last night. Wandering in the rain without any clothes on."

So that's what I was doing.

"Did someone find me?" I ask to help myself regain the collection of events.

"The homeowner of the house you were terrorizing sure did." There's that snarky tone of hers again.

And without my permission or even a warning delivered, the needle is jabbed into my arm. What looked like about 5 mg if I read it correctly.

"This is Haldol. You should feel more relaxed in just a moment."

I'm plenty relaxed. I don't need some drug. What does she think will happen?

And like the first day of snow fall, a slow layer of snowflakes begin to pile over my body. I'm numb. My responses are slower than they've ever been.

I look down at my body, and it's strapped to a gurney. My wrists and ankles are wrapped in cloth Velcro pads. I can't lift them past an inch off the surface.

I'm vulnerable right now. I've never been this open against an attack. Not having my physical ability to fend off pokes and prods is intolerable.

But…this would be a great technique to use on a bitch. I ponder if I can make these straps. While I'm wondering where I could find the supplies, or better yet how I could steal this binding equipment, I'm already being wheeled away, hallway after hallway. Into the depths of this facility that has become a labyrinth and impossible to keep track.

#

I've been taken off the hospital bed and sat on some couch by a large black man. I'm encircled by zombies walking by me. They're shuffling and leaning on the walls as they make their way around me. They don't pay me any attention but I'm watching each fucker as they pass by.

I don't have the energy or capacity to get up. To break out of this place. I'm zoned out without the ability to hone in on what I should do.

My jaw doesn't appear to work because it's slacking. I'm drooling on myself and trying to wipe it off my chest.

The weight of my head pushes my mouth down, but I work my neck muscles enough to lift my face up.

To let the humiliation of my current predicament really sink in, sitting right across from me on a smaller sofa is some petite girl. I recognize her bone structure but everything is a blur. She's staring right at me. I can't tell if she's smiling but I can see the straightness of her teeth.

I look around to see if anyone else is centering their attention on me. To my right is some old man yelling at what looks like a nurse in white. His hair is frazzled and he appears weakish but erratic at the same time. To my left is some old woman dancing to nonaudible music but obviously off rhythm because her movements are spasmodic.

Is that my future here? Where the fuck is The Board?

My feeble body is shifted to the right as someone just sat down next to me and made the couch cushion I'm also on indent. Like a slow revolving lantern on a lighthouse my head scans to my side to focus on who or what is pressing against my body.

It's the same fucking girl from across. God damn it she's fast.

She's looking right at me, close enough to examine the pores on my face. Near enough that I can smell the conditioner in her wet hair.

"I know you." The most alluring tone of voice whispers into my ear.

I can't talk, although I make a valiant attempt.

"Huhh?"

"I've seen you before." She barely explains herself.

"Mmm mmaa" I make another try at reciprocating communication.

"They really gave you the strong shit." She giggles in an honest tease.

She grabs my jaw with ice cold hands to rotate my head, left and right.

I jerk my face away from her.

“Aahh uhhhh” Trying to tell her to fuck off is fucking futile.

I’ve been reduced to a blob of human mass incompetent to the nth degree of fending off this tiny female that is having her way with my drugged up body. I’m livid but unexpressive.

“Easy lone wolf, I’m just checking the bruises on your face.”

My eyes are failing me now, rolling back into the blackness of my orbital bone and forward again toward the clouded scene before me.

“Your body is a lot harder than I expected.” She’s walking her hand over my arm, tip-toeing her fingers down the top of my forearm. She’s doing it slowly back and forth.

The same stabby nurse from earlier yells from another side of this large unit from hell.

“Leave him be, Eve! Let him get settled for God’s sake!”

So that’s her name.

“It’s ok! I know him!”

How does she know me because I don’t recognize her.

Where the fuck is the god damn Board when I actually need them for once.

#

I’m now in my assigned room after forced somnolence. I don’t remember how I ended up in this room, but I presume some large black man assisted my body into here. He better not have tried to butt fuck me.

Looking around for a reminder that this is truly my reality, I can see that the door has been left wide open. I was probably butt fucked.

My vision is no longer blurred; I can see clearly again. But my head doesn't feel light, it feels heavy. My thoughts are dense. They're not coherent, but lacking imagination of how to hurt others. I'm seething. I keep trying to refocus my thoughts on sadism, but I can only contemplate on getting out of here, on how to make it past these heavy steel doors with my fucking dignity.

#

An entire day later and I'm ordered to attend some ridiculous group therapy session. Sitting in a foldable steel chair, I realize that this entire facility is constructed of steel. The doors, the windows, the beds are designed to be resistant to breakage. It's been created for the housing of the most mentally unstable citizens of society that are apt to hurt themselves, or in my case others. And those that are a risk to society have a tendency to abscond whenever confined. Because I'm trying to get the fuck out of here. This place is supposedly break proof, but I'll be the test of that merit.

We're sitting in a circle, myself and 8 other patients. All here for different reasons, which is obvious by the idiosyncratic physical appearances of each. There's a few old folks that belong in a nursing home but I could also see these old fuckers ripping the place to shreds. They look like they've been malnourished for decades. Scattered about are several men and women that were likely homeless if not for being 5150'd by some doctor instead of being booked into a holding cell. To my adjacent right is some bald skinhead-looking asshole that is heavier than 10 black women. He doesn't belong anywhere and seems to be at the verge of losing his cool anytime. To my abutting left is a young woman which I can tell is a female by her quaking leg bouncing itself at an earthshaking pace that would break a baby's spine if sat upon.

It's the girl from my college class, the chatterbox during the lecture. The same bitch that was disturbing my personal space on the couch while I was degraded by chemical paralysis. This fucking chick is becoming a level-five clinger and I don't even know her name.

Oh yea, it's Eve. The origin to my living nightmare.

She's staring at me while everyone is giving their introduction. I'm trying to pay attention to the reason they were admitted, their given diagnosis, and how long they've been here. Apparently many of them have different sorts of hallucinations, and have been here longer than I intend to.

It's her turn to give her introduction.

"Hi everyone, you all probably know me already. I'm Eve, I've been here only 2 days, but this is my 7th time at Eloise. Oh and I've been diagnosed with Bipolar and Borderline, but that just means that I'm a people person and umm…I love hard." She spells out like she's said it a million times while making intense eye contact with me the entire time and biting the shit out of her lip.

Her gray eyes are piercing. She's not analyzing me for once, but penetrating into me in a way that is keeping my attention.

The therapist calls me out.

"Ryder, would you like to give us an introduction about who you are and what brings you into Eloise Hospital?" She interrupts our moment with a condescending voice.

"Uhh" I think of what I should say while distracted by the girl sitting up in her seat and leaning forward by supporting her weight on her two small palms.

"My name is Ryder. I think I've been here a day or two. And I don't have a diagnosis."

The entire cohort laughs in my face. Apparently my explanation has some humor in it, but I don't see it.

An obviously ill woman in her room snorks out loudly, "Sure buddy, and I'm Princess Diana!".

Followed by loud remarks from the cackle of hyenas.

"Easy Diane. We all remember our first group don't we?"

Her attempt to stand up for me is demeaning.

This group is fucking useless.

#

Being in my assigned room again offers me calmness. I've never been provided, much less forced to live in, such a clean and bright environment. The sanitary nature of this facility destresses one into a mind numbing lull.

But I saw an older pair sitting on a makeshift bench in the dayroom playing chess. I haven't played since I learned from my grandfather, but what better way to pass the time in such an inhospitable place.

Outside I wait for my turn. When it arrives I sit perpendicular to the board and set up the pieces in the correct arrangement. I intend to compete with myself, to make this a bloody battle with as many casualties as fathomable.

But lo and behold, not 15 minutes in and I am once again disturbed by the nagging voice of Eve, the one and only.

“Aren’t you a little too old to be playing board games?” she inquires with no inflection.

“This isn’t a board game. It’s an exercise in strategy.” I try to teach this chick a thing or two.

“I prefer to practice on people.” She’s smiling and again digging into my cerebrum with her gunmetal eyes.

I ignore her and her stare. She reminds me of my childhood, and that is not a place I intend to become reacquainted with.

I get up and walk away from the chessboard. Not wanting to engage with her is becoming a chore in the small confines of this unit. But regardless, she follows me.

I find myself pacing up the long hallway, away from the commotion of the common area. And yet against my approval, mayhem is close behind.

“So question! How has it been without the voices?”

Wait. How the fuck…

I stop in my tracks and turn my body about to face hers.

“What are you talking about?” I snap at her perfectly round face.

“I’m only assuming that’s what put you in here. And everyone says goodbye to their hallucinations when they first come in. So, how do you like it without the voices?”

“That’s not what put me in here.” She receives my gruff response.

I walk back down the corridor toward the dayroom.

“Oh I heard what you did. You were walking around naked with that hard body of yours!” She calls it out loud enough for a patient in her room to hear and snicker.

"How the fuck do you know that?!"

"People tell me things." She flashes that devilish smile again.

"But a better question you should ask, is did your voices tell me what you were doing…" she starts laughing her ass off.

"You need to stop and shut the fuck up."

"I can stop following you around or I can shut the fuck up. But I can't do both."

"What do you want from me, Eve?"

"Nothing really. I just want to be your friend."

"I don't have friends."

"Then one more reason why you need me as a friend."

What makes her assume I need her. I don't need anyone. Where in the fuck is the god damn Board…

I've made it past her but I'm cornered at the end of the hall. Standing in front of the heavy steel emergency door, facing away from her, my eyes are fixed on the grass just feet away from me on the other side of the tempered glass. Representing my freedom or lack thereof, a patch of grass that's greener than the olive pastel on the walls.

I turn around to face her.

"All I'm saying is, now that you don't have any voices, do you like it or do you miss them?" She's now right up against my body and asking me things while looking up.

"I don't. Have. Voices." I try to deflect her intrusions.

"I can always tell what everyone has. Some see things, some like me believe things, and people like you hear things." She serenates me with her subduing voice while licking her thick pink lips.

"I'm not a crazy motherfucker like you. I don't belong here." I try to evade her body and perky tits rubbing against my upper abdomen.

But she steps to the side to keep me here. "I've actually been called a daddyfucker, for your information."

She giggles while singing her quip like a siren.

I'm transported to walking in on my mother being fucked by someone's father. I don't want to be here. The Board needs to get me the fuck out of here.

"Step back or you're going to regret it. You know nothing about me."

She grabs me by the balls. Her small hands barely cupping both testicles but clutching it enough to push them up toward my body.

"Why aren't you understanding that I WANT to get to know you." She whispers through her small teeth.

And like a ride at an amusement park, she sends me to a distant place I don't want to revisit. I'm at that instance where another assertive woman cornered me and reached into my pants. Grabbing and putting all of it in her mouth.

"You need to get away from me or something bad is going to happen." I forewarn her of the inevitable.

"Bad like you'll let me be bad or you're going to treat me badly?" She spells off more of her riddles.

I don't understand most of what she says. She places me in difficult situations where I can't breathe. I can't think when she's around.

“Ol’ chap, sweetheart, fella. Ol’ chap, sweetheart, fella…”

“What the fuck are you doing?” She catechizes me.

“I…I…I don’t…where…” I’m trying to resurrect The Board.

I need some direction, some guidance. I’m able to make it past her by waving her body to the side.

Again, I feel like I’m floating on water but the wind has been removed from my sails. It’s taking all of me to keep my feet moving, left then right. Left step, lift the right and step. But against every intention to make it far away from her, my body lacks the coordination and I eventually begin to drop. Fortunately I’m able to see the wall to my left and reach my arm out to stabilize my fall.

Unbeknownst to me the wall I expected to support my weight turned out to be a door. Yet I fall through allowing my shoulder to catch my weight. I crawl toward a nearby desk as necessary reinforcement to sit myself up against. My back is resting on it so I can look at the open doorway.

My mind is racing but not moving. My hands are shaking but not doing anything. These eyes of mine are fixed on the ground and visualizing things not present.

A keen appreciation that I’m for once alone, truly alone, is starting to sink in deep. I have no one to look after me. No voice nor personality to care for me.

I’m without my talents and under threat of being controlled, by an outside force.

My soul is at peril for being sold to the highest bidder.

My heart here and there. Her soul reflected inevitability.
She's my remedy, my entirety, foreboding destiny.

Chapter 12

Soulmates

Without my knowledge, a hand is rested on my shoulder. I didn't notice anyone when I came in and I haven't seen anyone walk in.

I hear that familiar poised voice echo within the four walls to where I've been chased.

"There there. Easy big fella." She soothes me with a faux sentiment.

"What the fuck are you doing?"

"I don't know, man. I saw on tv this is what you're supposed to do when someone starts to panic." She smiles while saying it.

"I'm not panicking. I…I…" I'm tongue tied.

"It doesn't matter. I've got you." She puts her hand behind my neck. Holding it firm.

This is the first time another human has caressed my body with their hand. I've been sucked, fucked, and smacked around before. But never brushed like a pet. It feels alien.

Her light strokes give me a semblance of solace.

"Why do you keep following me around? Why do you keep fucking with me?" I have to ask while unable to make eye contact.

"Honestly, you look like someone that needs to be fucked with." She shows a glimmer of humanity behind her eyes, as if she meant it with tenderness.

"I don't know what you mean, but…I don't mind it."

"You don't mind me or you don't mind me rubbing your back?" There she is again complicating my existence.

"I don't mind your hand, I'm…not sure about you."

She doesn't look like someone that should be trusted. I have a thought that I doubt she would be qualified as a babysitter. She comes off like someone that would not only wreck a home but have a family turn on each other. And that turns on every fiber of me.

"Can I show you something? It's technically illegal though." Now she's speaking my language.

"What is it?"

Instantaneously she lets off her little weight from my back and grabs me by the wrist. Another sensation I'm not fond of because last time someone did that they were put in the hospital.

She stands up before me and pulls on me to follow her suit. I get up while scanning her legs to her torso. Her arms are lined with a multitude of scars, but all I can see are her freckles peppered about. She has a small waist and thighs meant to run. Her nipples are nudging past her issued psychiatric gown. I doubt she's wearing a bra, and if she's not, does she wear any underwear?

And within seconds of noticing her eyes watching mine survey her perfect body, she's pulled me into another hallway. This time into a break room that has been left unlocked. It looks like staff co-mingle here for snacks and refreshments. How did she know it would be unoccupied?

At the backwall, there's an emergency exit. Unlike the other in the hallway, this one has a push bar labeled in bright red: ALARM WILL SOUND. And to no surprise this bitch pushes it and sounds the loud ass alarm.

Still holding on to my arm like a toddler, she turns me around the corner once outside.

"Are you a good climber?" Her lips practically touch my chin as she smirks her forecasting question.

If she only knew that I know my way around a fire escape because I rape women for a living.

"Let's go." Her eyes widen once I give my approval.

And as the alarm is blaring and we can hear doors opening and slamming, staff voices are beginning to call out. They're yelling out commands in cooperation to find whoever is attempting to escape. Or in our case, those who are trespassing government property into very restricted areas. She's guided me towards a drop latter that she pointed at without saying a word.

Instinctually, I grab her by the waist and hoist her up so that she can grab hold of the lowest rung. She pulls herself up and I get a good look at a bottom view of her ass as it climbs, as it flounces from left to right. Her sweatpants have creased down the middle and inside her crack. She's definitely not wearing any panties.

I jump up once snapping out of it, and remember that there's an entire shift looking for us. Slowly pulling my body up, I notice that it's weaker than usual. I'm not climbing on adrenaline from the rush of hunting someone. I'm following the tail of someone who is not giving me full information of what we're doing.

And once on the roof of Eloise Psychiatric Hospital, she walks toward an access door in the middle. It appears that staff frequent this area because there's a chair next to it with cigarette butts overflowing an outdoor ashtray. She takes the metal chair and wedges it under the door handle to prevent anyone from opening it.

I don't imagine this is going to turn out in our favor because getting caught is inevitable. But I just want to keep following her lead and bear witness to what comes next.

She walks toward the ledge and waves me over. We're both standing straight, staring down at the small bodies running around. They look like ants scurrying throughout the hospital grounds, pointing, and communicating to find us out.

It's astonishing how people tend to keep their focus on what's in front of them, but never to look up. We stand there for more than a moment to test the theory that they'll never find us because that would require them to raise their perspective. To consider that we're more unpredictable than what is expected.

She orders me while suggesting with her finger, "sit down right here".

I sit on the ledge with my back facing the fall. She kneels down in front of me. On her knees and rests her icy hands on my thighs. To lean in so that she can kiss me.

She sucks on my bottom lip and forces my eyes to close. At any given second I expect her miniature hands to force my body back. To make me tumble, to complete this practical stunt with a plummet befitting of someone like me. Someone who's never been kissed with such adoration.

The plunge into gravity never arrives. Instead she sticks her tongue inside my mouth and flicks mine as if they're having a tongue war.

And right as I'm getting into it, forgetting the measure of time. Ceasing any regard that behind me a staff member will see us and seize us from ever finding freedom, she lets go.

"Pull your pants down." She demands just like I have, to many before.

I do as I'm told. And push the seam of my sweats down to my ankles inches off the floor.

"Try to relax."

It's demeaning that she thinks me an anxious mess. But if that's what it takes to have her stay enamored with me, I'll take it.

And more gently than I could have ever expected she flops my soft penis into her jaw. At first using her teeth to grab hold of it, and pull it fully immersed inside her throat.

She starts to suck on it, from base to tip, and restarting the process, back and forth. Slowly her wet mouth increases the lubrication. Making it easier to push my dick down the length of her tongue, and out again as it becomes engorged.

She grabs the lower third of it with her compact fist, and rubs the head side to side from one corner of her mouth to the other. She's releasing small bubbles of spit as she does this, causing drips of my precum and her saliva to trickle down her chin. She fits the head past her lips and sucks it like a lollipop making it plop out once her suction reaches the tip.

I'm fully erect. I'm for once fully, and utterly turned on.

It seems like she notices the rigidness of my dick because she lets go and places both hands on the graveled ground beneath us. Her ass is resting on the back of her ankles.

To push herself toward me, she moves her entire body forward to force two thirds of my penis down her esophagus. She leans in making her hair fall over her face. Her throat is making a clicking sound every time she rocks into me. Every time it hits the back of her throat. She coughs every few times she lunges me into her mouth.

The alarm isn't audible anymore. The staff's voices calling out aren't being heard any longer.

She's slurping and drooling all over it. I can hear the wet sounds and feel her warm saliva trickle down my balls. To get a better view I lean back, placing my hands on the very edge of the retention wall. My upper back is balanced past the ledge, with my legs spread out on both sides of her.

And in the corner of my eye, the handle of the roof access door is being turned. It's attempted to be pushed open, but the chair wedged below the handle is holding it shut.

Nevertheless, what Eve is doing with her mouth is more urgent. It commands more attention.

I groan out, loud, as her epiglottis is being rammed against with her weight jamming my dick inside her.

"Uugggh, fuck." I let out.

I've seen this move in pornos but I never imagined that the emphasis is not on the suction around my dick but on the pressure the head is feeling as it's being pressed against the back of her throat.

She scoots up to sit closer to me. Her knees are together as she's leaning over my lower body. She takes both hands and wipes the gravel rocks off against her pant leg, without skipping a beat, while keeping rhythm of her head bopping up and down. And with both palms she grabs the base of my cock again and stacks her other hand above it. In a synchronized movement she turns both her hands in opposing directions while she sucks the end of my dick like a vacuum.

I'm sure it's loud enough to be heard down on the ground, but I don't look back to take any notice.

Instead, I grab the back of her head. I grip a handful of hair because every inch of my dick is feeling beyond intense.

The door handle is still turning up and down, but with more haste. We both hear loud pounding coming from the other side because she stops to surface her head above water and look back at the source.

"Don't stop, I'm about to cum…" I grunt before pushing her head down with my grip.

She starts rotating her hands faster, pulling on my erection away from me, then twisting it back down. Although she's sucking the head and using her tongue to rub the bottom near the penis hole, she continues to let loose a good amount of slobber to moisten the friction. This hard rubbing of my genital skin makes me feel like I'm going to explode.

My toes are curling, my thighs are straightened tight.

"Fu…Fuck!" I moan.

The chair holding them back is being shaken as the door is being rammed against.

Someone under us is yelling at us. "Hey you!"

And without awareness of where I'm at and what's about to occur, I burst. I release everything inside me. I empty the semen being withheld inside my testicles, all of it right in her mouth.

It feels like time has elongated because with every convulsion, more fluid is shot inside her.

She doesn't stop rubbing me up and down. She doesn't slow as she flicks her tongue on the end of my dickhead. She's swallowing my entire load.

My eyes return from staring at the back of my head, and I catch her looking at me. She's smiling while wiping her lower lip.

We stand up in a hurry, not before I quickly pull up my pants from the seated position, and walk over to the door. Right before removing the wedge she reaches down and hands me a cigarette butt.

"Here, just say what I say, ok?" She instructs.

And right as we remove the door stop, the door is flung open, almost hitting her.

A large aid and the same heavy set nurse charge out, "What the fuck are you two doing?!"

"Ahh!" She squeaks. "We were just getting a smoke, we're sorry!" She performs.

Both grab us by the upper arms, and drag us back inside.

We were told to go wait in our rooms while they confirm we're the only ones missing.

Fast forward several hours, we're served dinner in our rooms. We're told that we've lost all our privileges.

That that was unacceptable behavior and our admissions could be extended if they find that we were attempting to kill ourselves.

But we weren't going to lose our lives just then. Instead I've been given life. I've been reformed.

I want more of that, more of her. I want to feel the other holes inside her body.

I need to learn about every inch of her body. I'm officially addicted to something other than killing.

I'm hooked on Eve. The first real woman in my world.

Her smell, her flavor, her fucking wild behavior.

We tell each other when we're discharged we'll continue this some more.

It trembled when he reached the summit.
The crest where love is established.

Chapter 13

Falling Off Mount Olympus

How is one supposed to focus on Mr. Whateverhisnameis when I was just released from a psychiatric institute? How can I pay attention in the very class where I first met that wildflower?

I'm in the same chair from when we first met. I'm watching the lecture but my focus is attended on the large wooden door.

I've looked behind me several times in case she's sitting right where she was, as she tends to appear out of thin air.

She should be showing up at any moment. Just as promised. We would reconnect and revive the thing which we started.

My mind is yet again racing.

I was discharged under the strict requirement of following up with a psychiatrist, which I have been scheduled for tomorrow at 2 p.m. I'm taking 2 milligrams of Risperidone and all of my voices have stopped since being admitted into the hospital.

I have yet to be reunited with The Board. I can only assume that they've left me to fend for myself. To leave me to my own sadistic devices. It's their loss.

I'm not on my laptop during class as I usually am. I'm not listening to a woman being mutilated. I'm not in any way attempting to hear what this bumbling educator has to say.

The thought of what she did to me, what she said to me is spinning circles inside my brain.

The way we caused trouble and got away with it is opening up a dimension of possibilities. She's a dangerous creature and I'm an artist at creating damage. We're a volatile mixture, a flammable compound with the potential to burn up some places.

She doesn't even know who or what I am. She's entirely unaware of what I do.

My thoughts are sprinting to the next possibility of sharing myself with her. I want her to know what I'm about, and I have a strange inkling that she'll be receptive to me after meeting the monster that I am.

I'm traveling through future spaces in possible times where we commit crimes together. Where we develop each other's creativity. Although we have the shared interest of rule breaking, our difference is in how we carry it out.

To say she's innocent in comparison to me is downplaying her capability. But I'm quite confident she can catch up to my speed. I'm positively certain we can find our rhythm. I want to teach her how to hunt women.

My line of thinking has become dotted and scattered. It's zigzagging from mental image to scenario. From running down bitches to birthing fires. She has the propensity to place herself in precarious situations without concern of capture.

There's so many lives available to destroy within such a short timetable.

The fire I caused on 30th street is replaying in my brain like a short film. I can still hear the choking and crying of an entire family.

I check the Casio watch on my wrist because I'm not able to stand up anytime in the near future. I'm rock hard and the more I think about the pain I've caused them, of what I've taken from them, the more my dick has leakage.

I have to show her the control I have over others. That I'm the devil reincarnated.

Eluding security to do sexual things is one thing, but to play god of fire and curse the lives of innocent men and women is a greater thing.

#

A week has gone by. No sign of my partner in crime.

I don't know where to find her. We never exchanged numbers.

I've circled the hospital several times per day in hopes that I would catch a glimpse of her gorgeous face. But every time I stop to watch the new crop of residents out in the yard, she is the only one missing. She's absent and likely to have already been discharged.

I don't know what she was in there for. She never told me. She mentioned she believes things. So would she accept the idea of me?

Why hasn't she come to class? If someone did something to her, I'll scorch the earth on which they reside.

I've shown up to class religiously. Although it's only three times per week. I'm the first to arrive and sit in my seat. Waiting impatiently and preparing what I would say the moment she reveals herself behind me. I'm the last to leave. The professor has now learned my name and asked to tutor me.

"Mr. Strickland, there are better ways to go about succeeding in this course than spending all your time in class."

"I just have a lot going on."

"You're better than a C grade. Stop by during my office hours, I'll connect you with my graduate assistant."

"No thank you. I'm doing fine."

I obviously declined because I'm passing his 200 something course with my eyes closed. College is a tedious requirement that I complete with ease. I don't need his fucking approval.

In between classes and returning to volunteer at the fire station, I've been revisiting my fire locations. I was also required to provide the station with my discharge papers, and I have a meeting with the Fire Chief for mental health accommodations.

I've since replenished my lighter fuel stash, and discarded the stolen jacket. I've repositioned some kindling material in carefully selected homes. The time away afforded me a period of rethinking my strategy. I've rechecked the door locks and some I've cracked opened to kick them down in anticipation of impressing her at the right time.

I'm having everything at the ready for when she joins me on my nights of planned arson.

#

Another week has passed. I'm going fucking crazy sitting on my thumbs.

But not the type of crazy that gets locked away, strapped down, and injected with antipsychotics. I'm itching to see her again so badly that I can't breathe. I've noticed my shallow breaths that I'm holding whenever I see another short girl with long brown hair.

I can't jack off anymore. I've done it so many times to the flashback of her sucking me off, that out of respect I've told myself to hold off until the real thing.

Instead I'm picturing fires.

Like Hephaestus, the Greek god, I've been rejected and deserted. I'm cast to a dark hole, destined to work on my equipment of suffering. I'm now responsible for cursing anyone undeserving.

I've decided to make a large fire as a calling signal.

Last time she caught me in the middle of losing my sanity. She presented herself at my loneliest moment.

I'm aiming that this time, as I'm controlling the chaos, she'll find a way to reappear. I know that she's attracted to madness.

So this will be an established opportunity for me to be rejoined by my Aphrodite.

To be reconnected with that which I find holy.

A relic of the devil's truest existence.

All that is good and bad.

Don't ever tame your demons.
But always keep them on a leash.

Chapter 14

Calcification

I'm standing in front of the chosen building. It's a larger home than the last one. And in the middle of a quiet suburb.

In my bag of tricks is a 32 ounce bottle of a charcoal lighter fluid. This won't be a slow cook. I'm going to fry this fucking community.

I'm in a black hoodie in a white neighborhood. Inconspicuous because I'm of their same color. But I don't belong here. My world is desolate and without warmth. Where their world is attractive and endearing. With signs of Halloween decorations on most houses and a set of birthday party balloons floating over a mailbox.

It's 1 a.m. and the block is empty.

Howbeit, in a few long steps and a hop over a fence, I've infiltrated the property. I plan on searing a permanent scar on the face of their pretty street.

The back door has already been unlocked, after my survey of the chosen properties a few days back. The front door is strapped by a lockbox that people hang up when selling a house.

Out of my pocket, I poke my ears with headphones roaring lighting shit on fire music, like Pantera – "Revolution Is My Name".

I slowly open the back door and a loud creak reverberates throughout the empty home. A straight path to the living room yields a track where I begin squirting the lighter fluid all over an old couch then onto the hallway leading into the stairs. They're covered in dusty carpet, as is a beat up rug under the sofa.

The dining room furniture, where a close knit family once broke bread, is removed as if it never happened. The table is flipped over on the doused living room floor and the chairs are stacked on top.

I proceed upstairs to continue spreading the flammable fluid on the ground behind me.

I walk straight to a large bedroom. It gives the impression where a mother and father would have rested their heads. There's a bed frame with a barren mattress on it. It's removed and dragged down the stairs. It's left there to ensure that a secondary sizeable fire is created to fetter the 1st and 2nd floor.

The line of liquid is continued into the entrance of each bedroom. Three bedrooms are met with a puddle of butane. The small shaggy rugs from both bathrooms upstairs are dropped at the doorway of each bedroom. They're coated with a liberal amount of lighter fluid as well.

This wooden structure doesn't stand a fucking chance.

A large rag which feels more like a soft towel, softer than mine at home, is taken with me back downstairs. I squirt the remainder of the contents from the bottle all over the dark towel.

In my pocket is the trusty zippo lighter. With a flick of the thumb, a small flame is induced and fanned underneath the wet cloth.

In less than a nanosecond a torch is invoked. Before it burns me and spreads the heat all over my sleeve, I throw it on the prepared pile of living room furniture.

It's magnificent. The blaze that's been raised. It's a candle compared to my rage. But it'll suffice as a beacon to call for her.

I'm forced to stand back because the wildfire is spreading faster than anticipated. It's taken a life of its own, slithering down the path I've designated.

It doesn't take long to find the stairs and it crawls up faster than a rat out of hell.

I can hear the sizzling and snapping of fibers as the fire overtakes the home. The upstairs is fully erupted because light is filling the halls.

It's time to leave and allow chemistry to do its thing. I need to find a good seat outside to watch my infernal conception.

Once in the backyard from whence I've entered, the fire almost follows me outside because its banging on the back windows. The interior has been quickly illuminated, hastily lit.

This large suburban home is holding back the heat for only a bit longer. I can practically feel it crumbling. Just like my dick, it's about to explode.

Before I can walk back toward the front of the structure, to a safe distance away from meddling eyes, the roof has been ripped open by the blistering heat. With it, cinders are pushed upwards and taken off course. Like spores of a carnivorous plant, they're scouring for a new source.

I'm both alarmed and in awe of what I have done. There's no way to stop it now. Its chaos unhinged and unguided.

The house next door and the house behind are now being coated by the same embers. Their roofs are kindling and no match against such an infectious fire growth.

It's a contradiction. The simultaneous stillness of this quaint community and the roaring spread of fire.

I don't have much time to appreciate the artistry before a similar crowd at last is beginning to form out on the other side, in front on the street.

I can hear yelling and calls for help. As I've returned and found a good hiding spot behind a shed, I can see shadows of the neighbors running around like ants outside a mound that's been disturbed. If any of these morons grabs a bucket of water, I may be found… laughing out loud.

The house to my left and the house behind me are now officially aflame. Their roofs remind of the time that I lit a cat on fire, with flames coming out of its top fur and her eyes wide awake. The houses are being ventilated to a rollover mixture of smoke and oxygen reaching pockets of particles still unburned.

Both houses' lights have been turned on and the loud knocks on the doors are echoed about. It feels like time has been sped up, fast forwarded.

The house's roof on the left has collapsed. The house behind is still holding back. It seems like the neighborly alarm was a success because a larger crowd has gathered on both lawns.

I'm not able to escape to safety out the front where I came in. Surely, a young man dressed in black emerging over the fence would expose my bad deed.

Between the shack and the other house in the back is a chain link fence. No neighbors have alerted that family of their impending doom. They're looking out their windows, and I can see the profiles of their damned heads. They're watching their counterparts' house burn down. And It doesn't occur to them to check on the very house in which they're occupying.

So I'm watching in pure relish as the fire over them has tripped and fallen off the shingles to the attached garage. Away from their line of sight. Developing beneath their realization that their lives are in real imminent danger.

It's broken into their first floor. I can only presume through a window or crack in the fortification of a wall. Just like the other targets, an incendiary plague is chasing them.

The original house is raging and scorching loudly. The fire must be 50 feet because it's towering over the two stories.

The house next door is quickly collapsing. Fire is ripping through it like an apex predator digging into its prey.

The house behind me is fully alive. I've counted three or four individuals scurrying back and forth from the glass openings of their ivory tower. Beneath them on the first floor is a brighter light emitting dark smoke.

The shouting and howling has begun. They're crying at the top of their lungs. I can hear begging and pleading for someone to help.

"We're stuck inside!!! HEEEELLLLPP!!!!" A grown man is wailing from overhead.

I can't look away. I refuse to move from my position.

The headphones in both ears are booming Mudvayne's – "Dig" to where my ears are vibrating.

I'm going to watch every second of this. I want to watch them die slowly, being cooked alive.

I can smell wood burning. But I've yet to catch the scent of flesh.

Finally another group of people are on the other side, in front of the back house. I can see them clear as day running the perimeter, searching for a safe way inside.

I'm forced to slip into the shed. I'm now surrounded on all sides by do-gooders. A few have run past me and cleared the metal fence. They seem to be confused about who and how to save first.

What better place to rub one out. What must be the man's wife is shrieking. That sound you hear in horror movies right before the damsel in distress gets stabbed to death. In real life it's overwhelming and unequivocal. It sends shivers up my spine and makes three drops of precum squirt out.

I'm tugging on it slowly and rubbing the head of my penis to savor the agony before me.

I notice the door of the shack is slightly opened. I close it up so I can only observe through a small opening. A small handle from the inside is barely enough for two fingers through and hold onto.

And as if irony is the theme of today's story, a hero appears and is checking around the shed. A large man tries the door on which I'm holding back. I quietly push my foot on the wall, against a two by four holding a panel in place. My other hand is still grabbing the tip of my dick.

He tries to yank the door out of my grip. I hold it tight and don't allow for any give to make him think a person is on the other side. That someone unfamiliar is in the wrong place at the most inappropriate time.

This asshole is wasting his effort. He's blocking my view. I swear to any fucking nonexistent god, that if miss the exact time of their deaths, I'm going to come back and do this all over again.

And right as I'm losing feeling in my hand, as I can feel the plywood door slipping past my clenched fist, Mr. Take-Action lets go. Making the door pull back and cause my foot to slip. With the commotion of the triple fire and people screaming, he must've not noticed. Because I could have sworn that he would perceive that I was the reason for the door not opening. But just as he appeared he runs off to find another way of saving this family in need.

And within seconds, I'm right at that point before one orgasms.

Yet, there it is. Not the smell of flesh but the stench of burning hair is in the air. And just like that, I have more than enough material to bust my nut.

Ironically, the music in my one eardrum is "Sober" – by Tool. I'm rocking my hips to the drums while I can hear the family's squealing in my other.

My grip around my cock is as tight as my clasp around the handle. I notice the door is shaking while I'm ejaculating all over the wooden panels. In my signature move I hope someone makes contact with my semen. I've given a gift to the world, apart from the ability to ignite buildings on fire and take the lives of innocent men, women, and children.

I've done what I came here to do. Now how the fuck am I supposed to get out of here?

More people are turning out, in their pajamas and robes.

I'm able to crawl out of the small space, and quickly jump over several fences.

I calmly walk out toward the sidewalk from a side yard several houses down. I expect everyone to be out, and too much horror is surrounding to pay any attention to someone like me.

I'm having the best stroll of my life after causing such terror, while the multiple sirens of an entire fire brigade are nearing the scene of the arson crime.

I parked at a local park several blocks away.

So I slowly circle the outskirts of the neighborhood with prediction that Eve will finally reemerge. She'll be called to this terrorizing scene. She has to, it's lighting up this entire side of town.

Any minute now.

I try make eye contact with every woman I see.

Come on.

Where the fuck is she?

Come quick, danger.
Our lives are in peril. Languished and untethered.

Chapter 15

Save Our Ship

After the dust has settled and I've washed the soot out of my skin, I haven't been able to relax.

If I thought I was having racing thoughts before, they were at NASCAR speed but now this is Formula One. I'm barely gripping onto the pavement.

My mind is bombing down like a missile without coordinates.

Although there's no rest for the wicked, this restlessness is keeping me in motion. Keeping me insane.

I haven't eaten a morsel or drank a drop of water in 60 hours. My bed has not been utilized nor have I reclined once. My antipsychotic medications have been neglected, just as I have college and the fire department for the past week.

Ya thought you'd get rid of us huh fella?! Farmer John is in a jovial mood.

"I wasn't trying to. They forced me to take those meds."

It would behoove you to be more careful when taking a stroll, ol' chap. Professor Marks counsels.

"I took back control. Just the way I fucked that family up."

You sure have proven yourself burning those innocents alive, didn't you my dearest? Mrs. Bathory congratulates.

The sense of accomplishment one feels after murdering is incomprehensible. I don't understand what I feel. I'm considering that I've found my life's purpose. My one true calling.

And yet…I'm the most alone I've ever been.

This isn't as enjoyable without sharing my spoils of victory with Eve. She would have loved this. The assertion I had, we would have had, over those uppity suburbanites would have watered her sultry mouth.

She didn't appear as expected. So it's a gentleman's charge to go find her. Like a fiend that's lost his pipe, I'm frantic without my medicine.

I won't take absence for an answer to what we should be. If she's dead or locked away somewhere then I need to know. I need a definitive answer. If she just used me to consume my ejaculate then I also deserve to know.

#

I've driven past and around Eloise Psychiatric Hospital at least five times each day in the past week.

I've waited outside at different wings of the facility in hopes I'd catch sight of her during rec time. No one that remotely resembles her has been spotted.

You'll find what you're in search for at the least obvious location. Mr. Solomon recounts.

"What the fuck do you think it is I'm doing then?"

Well look at who's wearin' his big britches. Farmer John instigates.

I'm on my way to the school. It's not on the day that we have class together, but I can only assume she would take more than one course at a time.

Pulling into the parking lot in front of the history department building, my body is overtaken with a cold sweat. The temperature is in the high 60's but I don't seem to be concerned about the weather. I'm concerned about what I'll say if I'm confronted with her incredible face. I don't know what I'll do if she isn't present.

I've been parked in this lemon of a car for more than an hour. I should just go inside. If I have to peer into each classroom door after door, like a mass shooter seeking out his school crush, I will.

As I'm nearing the main entrance my feet have been stalled in their path. I can't go in. Not yet.

You better scurry along, the professor is about to begin. Mrs. Bathory intonates.

I've taken a seat on the edge of an oversized planter. The flowers and bugs dwelling inside of it are irritating me. Stupid fucking buzzing around my ear, flying into my space.

Just as I'm swatting away some fly from my fucking face, an image to my left is irradiated. As if the dark clouds following me have parted and allowed for light to shine sufficiently through to guide me toward redemption.

There she is.

Walking from the very parking lot where I doubted my reason for being here. We actually shared a same path once again.

That isn't her. Mrs. Bathory distracts. *Don't call attention to yourself.*

"It is her."

She has her head down.

"Eve." I call out.

She hears me but it's as if her eyes haven't focused on me yet.

"Eve! Hey!"

She finally turns to the right and makes eye to eye contact.

"Hey Ryder, what are you doing here?"

"Waiting for you."

"What day is it today?" She asks while closing her eyes.

She looks like she's in pain.

"It's Wednesday. What's wrong with you?"

"Nothing. We don't have class together today. You have class today too?"

She's not slurring her words but dragging them out as if they weigh a ton.

"I just told you, Eve. I've been waiting for you. I've been looking everywhere for you."

"I just got discharged yesterday." She almost whispers while looking around her surroundings.

Who is she bloody searching for? Professor Marks is paranoid.

I'm not sure if someone fucked her up or if she's fucked up. I almost don't recognize her with how she's acting.

"Are you ok, Eve?" I can't hold back my concern.

"I'm…um.. I don't know."

"What happened to you?"

She's rubbing her arm like a junkie, while looking down to the ground.

This one here is a troublemaker. Farmer John warns but what the fuck does he know.

"They changed my medication. It's really strong." She tells me with her eyes half closed.

"Let's get you out of here. Where do you live?"

"Just a few blocks away. I'm staying with my grandmother."

"Did you drive here?"

"No, the bitch dropped me off."

No chance in hell that she can go back to my place. Not to that pigpen I call a home.

"Let's get you home. Come on."

I walk her over to my rust bucket.

She's standing by her door after I've unlocked it. As I'm walking toward my driver side, I notice she hasn't yet entered the rundown car. Is she concerned for her safety?

"I'm not going to hurt you…"

"I'm waiting for you to open the door for me." She whines her broken voice.

She must be really weak from the new psychiatric medication, that her grip strength has been taken from her. I know better than anyone how firm her grip can be. But nevertheless, I walk back around to pull it open. I've never opened the door for anyone.

Once arriving at her grandmother's small one-story house, she grabs me by my hand just like before and walks me around the back. This is my comfort zone, this type of entrance is what I know.

Her bedroom is on the left side of the small cottage. She slowly opens her window with a ripped screen girdling the frame.

"We have to be quiet, for another two hours. Until she thinks I'm back from class, ok?"

She's done this before. Mrs. Bathory disparages.

She crawls through like an experienced thief, and I pull through as smooth as I can to impress her. I barely land and lose my footing.

That was foolish.

Once inside, she sits me on her bed and subsequently flops onto her stomach. She's face down on the hard surface of this thin mattress. I'm unsure how she's breathing.

"I've stopped taking my medications." I try to whisper near her head.

She hoists her head up and looks over to me for the first time.

"You have?"

"Yes." I smile for the first time in a long time.

It's as if I'm making the formal introductions between her and my world.

"And how do you feel?" she asks interestedly.

"I'm fucking better than ever…I have my…" just as I was going to divulge the return of my voices my plastic Nokia begins to vibrate like a dildo in my pocket.

"Hey shut that shit off!" she quietly chides me to not alert her grandmother.

It's from a local number I don't recognize. Yet, no one has this phone number, except for the fire station.

I answer.

"Ryder Strickland?"

"Says who?"

"Says what? Son, this is Fire Chief Crassus from Engine 33. Do you have a moment?"

"Yes, yes sir."

Eve's grandmother starts knocking on Eve's bedroom door. She's raising her squawking voice asking about who she's with.

"Eve! Is that you? Who are you in there with!?" She yells while banging on the door.

Eve is staring at me with wide open eyes bloodshot with cracked capillaries.

"We have a recent fire in Huntington Woods. There's suspicion that it was started by one of our own. And you were one of the few volunteers that were off that night." I'm barely able to make out what he's saying over Eve's loud grandmother.

"What night?" I cover the phone with my hand so I'm the only voice he's able to hear.

"Ryder, can you come into the station today? So we can verify your whereabouts."

Eve is pulling on my shirt to make me end the phone call immediately.

"No problem, sir. I'll be right in."

I hang up and place the phone on Eve's bed.

"Eve! What are you doing back from school!" This bitch is yelling.

Dearest! You should shut that old cow's muzzle! Mrs. Bathory adds to the commotion.

Eve asks what that was about. "Who the fuck is that? You changed the look on your face."

"The fire chief. He thinks I started a fire in Huntington Woods."

"Eve!" Granny is hammering on the loose door.

"Did you?"

"Yes."

"When?"

"Early Sunday morning."

She starts showing a side smirk and her white canine as soon as I said it.

"I'm calling your case worker, Eve! This is outrageous!" The loud knocking finally ceases.

"Did anyone get hurt?" She perks up while sitting on her knees.

"A family was burnt alive." I tell her with a dead stare.

"O.K. You need an alibi, that's all." She hops over to me on her bed and leans her face into mine.

"Alright. What's my alibi?"

Her grandmother is back and hitting the door with a hard object. "Eve, I'm calling her right now!"

Eve's hands are on my chest and I can smell her captivating breath. "You were looking after me, your girlfriend, when I discharged. I was supposed to discharge on Saturday but I didn't because my bitch grandmother was getting her oil changed."

"Can we prove it?" I try to get confirmation.

"Prove that I'm your girlfriend? I don't know, can you?"

"I meant, that I was with you."

"I know, dumdum. My liver enzymes were almost toxic on Saturday. Like 1.4, which is another reason I didn't discharge until I did."

You're barking up the wrong tree, lad. The chief is going to see through this charade. Professor Marks attempts to redirect me.

"But they'll check with the Eloise hospital on when you actually left. They'll catch me lying."

"That's the beauty of it. I technically discharged on Saturday but I waited all day and an agency nurse let me sleep in my same bed. I was picked up Sunday night."

"Alright. I'll do it."

#

I'm sitting in the chief's office. Across from him with a chipped desk between us. My fire sergeant is sitting behind me recording every word that is spoken. Another man in a white polo is standing in the corner with notepad in hand. He must be the fire marshal.

"Where were you on Sunday, Ryder?"

"Which Sunday?" I was prepared for that question.

"Two days ago." The team sergeant says behind.

You're being watched like a hawk! The farmer warns me.

"I was with my girlfriend all weekend. I was looking after her after she was just released from the hospital." I tell the group while turning in my chair.

"Do you have eyewitnesses that can confirm this?" The Chief inquires further.

"I do. Ask the hospital and I can give you her number or address. Whatever you prefer."

"We'd appreciate that. I also understand you were the first on scene at a fire on 30th street?" The Chief coldly asks me.

"I was. I live near Belleville Lake, and I was fishing nearby, at the river."

"You were fishing at Detroit River at 11pm?" The guy in the polo finally speaks up.

"Yes sir. That's when the fish are biting."

"How long were you there before Sergeant Briggs?" Chief redirects my attention to him.

"About 5 minutes."

"The dispatch transcript said you said you'd be there in 10 minutes, but the team arrived on scene in about 7 to 8."

"I was leaving my fishing spot and heading toward a friend's house who lives in Dearborn." I think on the spot.

The marshal in white steps forward, "We've also learned that you were admitted into a psychiatric facility, after you were found spraying a house down butt naked at midnight".

"I don't really remember much about that night. I didn't know about spraying a house down."

The Chief takes lead again, "This is a formality. We're following whatever lead, as improbable as they may be."

"Thank you, Ryder. Please make sure you bring by those discharge papers, asap." Sergeant Briggs adds.

"Yes sir."

They won't be getting those discharge papers, because I threw it away upon my exit of the facility.

They diagnosed me with schizoaffective disorder. I don't know what that means, but I sure as fuck don't have it.

My mother is a schizophrenic, and I'm nothing like her.

She's weak, and I'm not. She was put away, and I'm never going back.

The system's curiosity doesn't get quenched with just a drop of untruth. Mr. Solomon advises, but what the fuck does he know.

Whatever the case. I live to kill another day.

Eve was right, this worked.

I can evade capture without strain.

They sure ate that shit up, didn't they? Farmer John congratulates.

We make quite the team, Eve and me.

We're treacherous. We're untouchable.

We're Styrofoam and gasoline. Like napalm, we'll fucking deep burn anything in our way.

If being hysterical is comical.
Then my instability is dry humor. Cruelty delivered as a practical joke.

Chapter 16

Lunacy

What if the fire marshal follows up and speaks to the temp nurse about Eve's true whereabouts? Mrs. Bathory complains in my ear.

"He won't. He bought it."

How can you be so certain, ol' chap? Professor Marks is questioning my confidence.

"Because Eve is my alibi!"

I'm yelling at the open air ahead of me while driving to my college course. From time to time the rearview mirror is the outlet of my aggression, but that makes me swerve in and out of the two lane road I'm traversing.

Look at ya! Callin attention to yourself like a coon' in a trashcan! Farmer John is being annoying as fuck.

I've finally arrived and pulled into the college parking lot.

You're here for an education but you refuse to learn from what we're instructing. Mr. Solomon has also turned on me.

I go to reach for the car door handle, but I'm still buckled in. I catch sight of my face in the rearview of sweat beading down my temples.

You're in no condition to go in there, my sweetest. Not after what you've done. Mrs. Bathory intercepts my exit.

"And what exactly have I done? No one knows nothing!"

The board isn't helping, they're bothering me. Trying to get a rise out of me, but I have shit to do.

I don't think it wise to show your face in there. Marks pesters me again.

My phone starts vibrating off the hook.

It's Eve.

Somehow I've allowed time to pass right by me. It's 30 minutes after class has begun.

You better not answer that, lovely. She'll come out and find you. She'll give away your position. Mrs. Bathory confuses me.

"And what fucking position is that?! I'm in the position of control!"

Says the youngin' yellin' at himself in a hot car.

He's right. I'm alone in here, while she's in there.

They're in the way. But they weren't when Eve and I met. When she deepthroated on my dick.

"Fine, we're leaving."

Where are you off to now? Professor Marks is now getting loud.

"Back home." I yell while the veering in and out of traffic hasn't improved.

To do what, my beloved? Lady Bathory is feigning concern.

"You'll have to see."

My phone hasn't stopped vibrating. Eve is probably concerned that I've been apprehended. But I can't answer her, not right now.

Once in the trailer, I walk straight to the bathroom. It's still stained crimson red, with red crust lining the grout between the laminate and shower.

I've found the bottle, full of a 27-day supply remaining, and I try to get past the child safety cap.

It slips in my hand and plunges down to the hard floor. Quickly picking it up, I try again. My fucking hands are shaking.

What in the Hootenanny do you think you're doin'?!

The bottle is thrown out of the bathroom and across the thin hallway. It doesn't shatter but disappears under some furniture.

Fuck this, I'm leaving.

#

I've decided to go see the psychiatrist the hospital scheduled me with. My follow up isn't for another three days, but I need something in the immediate sense.

I pull in to the first parking space I see. One at the very front with a pole and blue sign attached to it. But I don't have time to read.

Look at this joker, ya really do think yer disabled. Farmer John keeps fucking with me.

I walk inside and right up to the receptionist just feet away from the front door.

"I need to see the psychiatrist."

"Good morning. Do you have a scheduled appointment with Dr. Kraepelin?"

"No I missed my appointment with him a few days ago?"

"Ok no problem. Have you ever been here before?"

"No. I just really need to see the psychiatrist."

"Ok you will. I'm just going to need some information."

"What type of information?"

"Can you go have a seat? And I'll be over there in just a second." She points at several chairs behind me.

"Seat, over there?" I point to an empty chair in the busy waiting room.

I didn't realize there were any people in here until I just looked around.

She nods, "Yes, make yourself comfortable and I'll bring over some paperwork."

I find an empty seat away from the individuals waiting by another door leading to the back.

She doesn't take but a minute before she sits in the chair right next to me. She's holding a wooden clipboard and pen.

She smells like strawberries.

"So, let's start with your name."

"Ryder."

"I love that. What's your last name?"

“Strickland.”

“My name is Brooklyn. So you missed your appointment, did you schedule it or did someone else schedule it for you?”

“The hospital did. I was supposed to come in a day or two after discharging.”

“Oh ok. That makes more sense.”

It makes sense because she's judging you, dearest. Mrs. Bathory tries to influence me.

“I wasn't able to come in because I was responding to a fire.”

You've gotta be kidding me! Farmer John reacts negatively in my head.

Honestly boyo. Are you trying to get nicked?! Professor Marks is also mad.

“You're a fireman?! That's like one of the sexiest jobs around.” She looks down at the papers she's filling in immediately after saying it. “Sorry, that just came out.”

“I don't feel right. When can I see the psychiatrist?”

“I just need your date of birth, and I'll look you up in our system.”

“February 13th, 1987.”

“Oh my god, my daughter was born on February 14th!”

I don't know what to say to that. And in my mental uncertainty, I notice the redness in her hair, the green hue in her orange eyes, even the orange freckles sprayed on her nose. She has an athletic body. Does she work out daily?

“What's your home address in case we need to mail you your meds?”

"Lot 9, Eisenhower Street, Belleville."

"We're pretty close to each other. I live in Heritage Park with my kids."

"You live there with your children?"

"I do, but me and my ex share custody."

I eventually get to see the condescending Dr. Kraepelin, being kept in the back. I tell him that I hear things, to which he has no observable response. I describe that they talk to me every day and instigate me, that they make lose control. And he kept repeating that he understood, which I wholeheartedly doubt. That I don't feel like myself lately, and I just want to return to work, to get back to school. Which he said we all do. No the fuck we all don't.

He prescribes me a different medication I don't recognize among the several that have been pumped inside of me, but before he does he asks me impertinent questions.

"Do you have any thoughts of hurting yourself?"

"No." that's an easy answer.

"Do you have any thoughts of hurting others?"

I take a moment to consider all of the people I've hurt in the past few months. The people I hope to hunt with Eve at my side.

"No."

"Are you sure? You took some time to answer the question."

"I wouldn't hurt a fly."

To live a life full of lies only entangles you in your own web. Mr. Solomon isn't helping.

"This medication might make you feel very drowsy, so be sure to take it at night."

This quack wants to drug you just like they did before. Little do they know that's exactly what I need right now.

"Ok."

#

I take the medication as soon as I step out of the building. To rid myself of these demons. So that I can get back to what I do.

I'm in my vehicle driving back home.

There isn't any way you'll ever get us out of your head. Mrs. Bathory sounds more serious than ever.

"I need to get back to normal."

You ain't fuckin' normal. Yer as loopy as a crosseyed cowboy! That redneck John is a real motherfucker.

Just as I'm beginning to get into it, with my own thoughts in the rearview, my phone begins to vibrate.

It's the fire station. Obviously I answer immediately.

"Hello."

"Hey Ryder, how are you son?"

"Good, Chief. How can I help you?"

"Well that's just it. We're going to put you on medical leave. Until we review your records and conclude this investigation."

"I thought you said it was just a formality. That I was good to go."

"Oh it's a formal investigation alright, but we never said you were good to go."

"But I gave..."

Before I can finish he cuts me off, "I know you're supposed to be on call this evening but don't worry about it. I'll let you know when you're back on. Understood?".

"Yes sir."

I can't fucking believe this shit.

#

I'm sitting on the hood of my car, tossing with the pictures of my memory. Playing back, over and over, the conversation I had at the station. Inspecting for any cues that I gave myself away.

I'm on the outskirts of the airport, parked right against the fence.

If you believe in chance, boy, then you've got a real high probability of having a serious problem. Professor Marks isn't a fucking statistics professor, he studies bagpiping.

"What are you Scottish now?"

It's not wise to question our authority. Mr. Solomon attempts to embark some bullshit wisdom.

Every time I get some traction on focusing what I did to that family and what they'll find out about me, the image, the smell of Brooklyn leaches into my brain.

She's not good enough for you, my sweetness.

"You said the same about Eve." I refute.

I'm wondering when exactly she won't have her kids around.

What I do know is where she works, and I almost know where she lives.

I'm going to find out what makes her break. What makes her scream.

I'm going to rip her pussy to shreds.

Before it's all said and done, she'll be sawed in quarters and halves.

She'll be buried under a bridge.

Discarded like trash, like waste disposed of and returned to the earth.

As she deserves.

I shot dread in the head, took the bread and the lamb spread.

Chapter 17

Brooklyn

I've been in front of the psychiatrist's office since 2 pm. It's now 4:45 on a Friday afternoon.

I'm parked on the street across. My seat is fully reclined in case anyone, like Brooklyn or the psychiatrist, walks out and recognizes me.

Eve has called me multiple times, but after the sixth time she's given up. My phone hasn't been called for two hours and I have the entire evening open to do what I please to whomever I want.

I've enjoyed the quiet. The privation without The Board.

Slowly around 4:55 the psychiatric staff begin to file out, one by one. Several women in nice clothing and heels, a few men in button up shirts and dress pants. But no one that looks like the redhead I just met.

It's 5:02 and still nothing. Several lights inside have been turned off. It's a long building with multiple office windows. Someone in scrubs just walked out and locked the front door. It's not Brooklyn. It's some bitch in blonde.

Is she not working today? I knew I should've been here at 7 am to watch everyone file in. Just as I'm losing hope, just as I turn on the car ignition to drive away, several small cars drive out from the back parking lot.

There she is!

A person with small shoulders and a freckled face with her windows down. Her curly red hair is waving out of the vehicle in the breeze, shining under the setting sun.

Time to find out where she rests her head, to where she calls home. So I can plan my attack, at her moment of most vulnerability.

She drives fast. She's hard to tail. Several left turns and multiple rights later, and she's barely slowed down once entering a residential street. Does she know that I'm following her?

She's just pulled into a small driveway in front of a small house. I hold back about half a block to park alongside a curb. Two small children, as she mentioned, run outside to hug her. What a quaint family.

#

About four hours later, and I haven't seen much activity coming out of her miniature abode.

The lights are on, but the blinds are closed. No one has walked out since she's walked in.

I'm considering going in but it wouldn't be prudent. Although if The Board were present I'm sure they would be pressuring me to commit the crime tonight, even with the children inside.

It's not that I have an aversion to hurting the underage, it's that their screams would surely alert the neighbors and ensuing authorities.

It's going to be a long night because I don't want to leave and miss watching her go to work. I need to monitor her from when she wakes up, however early it may be. And if I miss her then I won't know where to find her if she doesn't go to work tomorrow.

#

It's Saturday morning. It was a long uncomfortable night. The neighborhood is now waking up. There are people outside cutting their grass, getting into their vehicles, but none have noticed me spying on their private lives.

A child opens her door and walks to the car. Brooklyn follows while holding her other child loosely in her arms. In her other hand is a large bottle with a smoothie filled to the rim.

She's wearing work out clothing. Small running shorts and a tank top. Her sneakers are white Chuck Taylor's. I know that because I owned a single pair for several years as a kid.

Following her after she leaves, she drops off her children at some guy's house a few miles away. He walks out to greet them, but doesn't touch her. I watch her run several errands afterward. It's been several hours, and she's finally arrived at the gym for which she's dressed. It's also a Gold's gym but at a sister location. As she works out I consider for several minutes the risk and reward of walking inside to pretend to work out while I watch her do her thing. Although my barcode tag would work, she would either become suspicious or the cameras would capture my face on the day of what I'm going to do to her.

She works out for about two hours. While leaving she's distracted with earphones popped in, but I have to restrain myself from making a move out in the open. Her obviously sweaty body is tempting. I wonder if her pussy smells as I think it does. Musky.

#

It's now 6 pm. Saturday evening. She's returned straight home without grabbing her interfering kids. The lights are on and music is streaming out of the closed windows. She's having her me time. She deserves it, and the better her mood is today the more this will hurt tonight.

#

It's now midnight. The lights and music have been turned off for a couple of hours, as well as any sign of activity has now ceased. I want to be certain that she's not awake nor in any state to respond to my unwelcomed entering of her premises.

I slowly walk out of the vehicle that has been my cage. My back is stiff and I can't help but stretch out my spine. My legs do that shaking thing, followed by a loud yawn. This community is oblivious to the monster hanging around.

I'm wearing sweatpants and a sweatshirt with nothing underneath. I'm prepared to break a sweat while breaking her.

Sneakers to make a fast escape if the situation calls for me to flee. A baseball cap to hide my face from any eyewitnesses.

In my hand is my bag of torture equipment. Inside is duct tape, my saw shovel combo, an old bike lock I haven't used in years, and a small boning knife to carve flesh from bone.

I've made it to the back of her house. She has no fence and no flood lights for the backyard. I quickly make it to her sliding glass door without being seen. I quietly yank on it with no expectation that she would grant me a lucky break.

It's fucking open!

I push it sideways to open it slowly. I step inside and watch out for any objects or toys left out on the carpet.

There's a light on coming from one of the bedrooms down a hall. It's a blue haze from what looks like a tv screen.

I'm ready, this is it. My bag is clinched tighter, closer to my chest. I walk toward the light. I'm stepping as softly and carefully as possible, as to not awake my sleeping beauty.

3…2…1! I rush past the doorway of the lit up bedroom. I'm already out of breath from the adrenaline spiking my system.

She's dead asleep. On her side, facing away from the bright box. No wonder she didn't wake up when the patio door scraped open.

Gently placing the bag down, I quietly zip it open to remove the large roll of metal colored duct tape.

I'm standing over her, appreciating the arcs and bows of her athletic shape. She's wearing a large t-shirt and hip hugging panties. It's giving her cream colored ass half a wedgie. Her arms are together under her face supporting the weight of her head.

Leaping in the air, diving over her still frame, I belly flop right on top of her.

Scaring the fuck out of her she yelps upon waking, “AAAHHH!!”.

I have to move quick.

Her long hair is wrapped around my fist twice. Her head is forcibly pressed down hard into the pillow. She’s squirming beneath me, trashing her arms and legs while letting out screams of terror.

“AARRRHH!!!” she yells her pretty voice while lifting her frizzled redhead with all of her strength.

Both of her hands instinctually have found their way over mine. She’s trying to rip my fingers apart from her tangled hair.

There’s my open window of opportunity. As she so badly wants, her hair is let go. Instead I grab her small wrists in my hand. The other and my teeth are de-rolling the gray tape. I revolve it around her two forearms up to her palms, about six times.

“OH MY GOD!!! FUUUUUUUU!!!”

Her face is dunked down, again, into the thick cushion. Suffocating this beautiful bitch.

Her legs and now conjoined arms are trying to raise herself, to push me off her back. Like a bull that’s been gored.

The pillowcase under her is unsheathed from its feather sac and placed quickly over her head. Immediately she tries to remove it with her fastened hands. The duct tape is once again wrapped around her neck about six times.

“PLEASE, PLEASE DON’T FUCKING DO…!!!

A punch to the back of her left ribs is hard enough to shut her up. Now she can’t breathe. She’s gasping, hoping for air.

Her panties are removed, and that really gets her agitated. She starts kicking around like a mule who’s had his throat slit.

She needs to be spanked into submission. I start wailing on her ass and lower legs. Smack, after smack, after smack, after smack. Repeatedly and with more vigor each time. It's too dark but her skin is making a loud clap as I pulverize the meat around her lower back, ass, and upper thighs.

The fucking screaming again, "EEEEEEEHHHH STOP!!! OW STOP!!! PLEASE!!!".

For being such a hard body this whore sure begs like she's weak. But the yelling needs to end.

Her mouth is wide open, noticeably from the imprint made under the cotton covering her face.

The roll of construction tape is put to use again, as it's wrapped right over her mouth onto the cloth. Tightly revolved six times to ensure she can't close it, but instead gag on the fabric she uses every day.

Her scent of freshly washed hair is filling the room. Her body is almost bare, but I've already felt her gentle skin. She's starting to sweat down her back.

This oversized shirt, what looks like a man's shirt, is in the way. My knife is the right tool to remove what she has left.

As I get off her stiff body she immediately starts tossing her body from side to side. She's pulling at her cotton mask.

"PA! PA! PEEEE!!! UUUUGGGHH!!!" she keeps trying to call for attention.

The back of the blade is pressed against her head and my lips are over her ear, "if you keep screaming this knife is going to be shoved in your ear. Nod your fucking head bitch!".

She nods her fucking head.

"I'm going to rip your asshole in half."

She starts bawling, “UUUGHHUUUGHUUUHHH!!”.

In two slices, the sharp knife cuts through the back of her shirt like paper.

She’s sobbing under the pillow cover, with long wails because she can’t close her slut mouth.

I drop the knife and give her six additional smacks to that perfectly chiseled back. Open handed and heavier than before. Each time, her body is bounced in the air like a basketball. With every hit she grunts.

It’s time to get started.

I take off all of my clothes. They’re laid out on her bedroom floor in case I have to put them back on and make a break for it.

She’s picked up.

More like lifted by the neck with my two hands strangling her, intertwined at the tips.

Her body is in the air, and she’s holding on for dear life on one of my wrists.

I’m suspending her above my head as she’s kicking me and trying to break free. At some point she’ll have to stop fighting. She’ll have to focus on breathing.

And just as her body is losing its strength, she wraps her legs around my waist and tries to prop herself up so that the grip around her throat doesn’t make her pass out.

I push my head under and in between her secured arms so that her hands are now behind me. Her restrained arms are resting on my shoulders but she’s trying her best to push herself as far away from me as possible.

"UUUGHHHH!" she groans loudly while spreading her cunt in front of me.

And like that I'm the most turned on I've ever been. More than when I was with Eve. Because a perfect specimen is masked tight, bonded at her upper extremities, and fighting for her life by holding herself in the air with her legs around my hips. My large hands are still crimping her neck like pliers around a thick water hose. And I can hear her struggling to suck in air to stay awake for what I'm about to do next.

My dick is hard, and because of its weight from being filled with pulsing blood, it's fully erect pointing forward right under her. In one single move, I dip myself under her pelvis and stab my penis into her, halfway inside her vagina.

Now she's really crying, "MMMOOOO!!!!".

But it only makes me raise her body up and lower it down to further my dick into her dry pussy. After a few thrusts, and I mean about 10 hard clashes of my hips into her pelvic bone, it's beginning to loosen up with more liquid between us.

To make sure she keeps her legs tight around mine I choke her harder to make her head feel like it's going to pop off.

I'm about to cum so I push her up above me and throw her off. She lands partly on the bed with her back plopping on the mattress and her legs slam against the bedframe.

Grabbing her by an ankle I drag her to the bathroom inside her bedroom. She's on her stomach now and likely burning her nipples while being rubbed across the thick carpet floor.

The light is flipped on. She has a shower curtain, and serendipity has appeared twice now in one night. The rod is drilled into the wall with three metal screws going through a metal faceplate on each end.

But it won't be used before her meat is pounded a little more. She's on her stomach and propping herself on both elbows. Her feet are pointing back and her knees are closely tight. Her whole body is stiff and she's starting to crawl away from me.

A cup being used to hold her toothbrush and her children's toothbrush is dumped out and filled with cold water.

It's poured on her bare back slowly before I yell my command, "Get on your FFFUCKING knees!!!"

She hoists her body up and gets on her knees, but her knees are tightly pressed against one another. I grab a single ankle and stretch out the thick tape. After cutting out three strips of tape approximately 12 inches long, I flatten them out over the back of her lower calf, against her Achilles heel. It's rubbed against the hard bathroom tiles to make sure she can't move. I spread her other leg open and repeat the tape flattening process.

She's sobbing loudly and vibrating in a panic.

"Aahh Aahh AH AAAHHH!" she can't believe this is happening to her.

She's now on all fours with hands bound tight and knees strapped to the floor of her home.

My dick's stiffness hasn't let up and it's been leaking all over her bathroom.

I slowly insert it into her vagina to make sure she savors every inch of my unusually thick penis. Her body pushes forward and away from me. The piledriver position aims my dick down toward the inside of her clitoris.

"UUUUUHHHHHHH!!!!"

I reach over to grab the U-shaped bike lock. The key already inserted releases it to open the curved steel. The bent shackle is placed under her chin and pushed into the crossbar until it clicks. Her cold handle is being pulled upwards and making her back arch.

She's gargling and holding herself on the ends of her tiny fingers.

My dick is fully inside. My body is slamming into her backside making the skin over her wide cheeks and lower back ripple. The red welts are now visible and raised, so why not break the skin?

In between bumps I crack her wet ass, making the hits louder. The skin over my palms is stinging so I can imagine her pain. I raise my right hand over my shoulder and swing down as loud as I can, into her ribs.

With each hit, her body tenses up, making the muscles inside her pelvis clench around my cock. But then, I'm close to climaxing again! I pull out quickly to not finish this prematurely.

My knife scratches around her ankles and releases her from being bonded to the hard floor.

By plucking her off the ground with my hands under her armpits, she's now standing on her feet. There's a huge wet spot where her face is. She's sniffling loudly. Her knees are bright red and finger marks are showing around her sides.

She's no longer crying, but shaking her entire body under her breath. "PA. UGH. PA. PEE PEEEGH".

I lift her body in the air with my arm around her torso and give her some direction.

"Grab the fuckin' shower rod!!" she jolts at my scream, and raises her hands up.

Both wrists taped tight grip onto the metal pole. Her small bare feet are standing on the edge of the bathtub. She's a balancing act.

The lock is detached and pushed up toward the shower rod with her neck still inside of it. It's secured over the metal bar. She instantly starts choking. Her hands are holding herself still but her feet are slipping with all of her fidgeting. If she was freaking out before, she's hysterical now that she's being lynched.

Let's raise the ante.

A large nine ounce bottle of shampoo is behind her, still wet from being used earlier today. It's rubbed over her clit, and slowly driven into her wet vagina. She initially fights being impaled but her legs spread out from the excruciating pain. It takes almost all of my strength to push it past her fat pussy lips to where her body is lifted. Her labia minora is small and the color of her light pink lips. Her labia majora is thick and the same color of her nipples, the lightest shade of red. The bottom edge of the bottle is finally crammed into her hole, and driven further, without slowing down.

It's now up to my knuckles and more than three fifths inside her.

"AAAAHHHHHH!!! AAAAAHHHHHHHH!!!!!"

Her upper body is shaking uncontrollably, but her lower body is fully tense.

Her asshole must be so tight.

I step up to her level. My dick is still wet from her moist pussy. The shampoo bottle is wide and I'm still holding it with my arm around her waist. My rock hard dick gets shoved into her rectum, against the large cylinder inside her front hole. It's so tight because I have to fight against the plastic, I'm stuffing her like a straw stabbing a paper cup.

I only get 10 thrusts in. Until the head of my dick grinding into her now enhanced vaginal hole starts to feel extremely hot. My penis head is engorged and about to burst.

To ensure this is a memorable experience, the boning knife is picked up off the bathroom counter. While fucking her anus and pushing against myself from the inside with a large plastic bottle, I rub the sharp end against the inside of her left bicep.

"AAAAAAAAAGGGGGGHHHHHHH!!!!!!!"

I slice her brachial artery. She's feeling everything.

Her sphincter being ripped with every thrust. Her vagina being stretched as it did when she gave birth. Her arm being cut deep with a cold blade.

Instantaneously, her body is swinging about. Blood, literal pints of blood, is squirting out like a cheap movie scene. Her body's dark red liquid is almost boiling hot as it cascades down her body. It even gushes over me and I can feel her life flowing down my knees. Somehow with the excitement coursing through both of us the bottle is too slippery to hold and it's pushed out.

Her other arm Is slashed open. Her bicep muscle Is cut almost all the way through in half. Her once white body is now ruby red and the waxiness of the blood is shining against the bathroom light. Her feet have slipped off the shower rim and her body is being suspended by the metal lock around her throat.

She's almost unconscious and I'm about to bust. It's now or never.

She's making faint noises, not crying but barely breathing out hard sighs over the metal noose.

I pull out almost all the way, withdrawing out the muscles of her blood lubricated asshole and stab her rectum again. Over, over, and over, and over, and over.

As she lets out of her gagged mouth a loud death sigh, I finally ejaculate. My whole body is tightened and I can't keep my eyes open. The knife is dropped and I hold myself up by grabbing her head cover with her sweaty hair inside it.

I moan loudly, “UUUHHHH FFFFFFUCCK”.

I slip after shaking both legs berserk and catch myself on the blood flooded floor.

I’m out of breath. I can’t breathe.

I feel like passing out, and possibly vomiting.

I've sold my soul to Satan. And returned my investment in blood. I'm paid with her hate. Earned in her trust.

Chapter 18

A Little Adorable Acid

I wash myself of her lifeblood in her children's bathtub. It's now also stained red.

Her blood is thick and under my fingernails. I haven't given any effort to rub it off, because I'll probably use it later for research purposes.

After drinking some water from the sink and calming down my nerves, I grab my phone from the pants on her bedroom floor.

The only person I can think of calling is Eve.

She answers only after two rings, "Hey Ryder".

"Hey."

"Is everything ok, baby?"

"I need your help, can I get you here?"

"Sure, I can be ready in 15."

#

I leave Brooklyn's dead quiet home the same way I came in. The bag of equipment is left for when I come back. I slowly walk over to my car and drive away without turning on any headlights.

I'm at Eve's house within 20 minutes, and she sneaks out of her window to meet me down the street.

On our way back to Brooklyn's I try to explain everything.

"So, is her body still hanging there?" She has the widest smile I haven't seen in forever.

"Yes. Attached to the shower rod."

"And you haven't cleaned any of the blood?" I have trouble understanding why she's so happy and taking all of this so calmly.

"No. I just showered in the other bathroom."

"That was smart calling me."

#

Once we get to her house she follows me in. I watch her walk past me and head straight for the kitchen sink.

"Yes! She has some." She exclaims again showing her teeth.

She's holding a large bottle of vinegar and walks right toward the hall of the murder scene.

I watch her pour vinegar over the children's shower and again in the bedroom on the bed and floor.

She walks into the painted bathroom and stands still for a while, staring at my work. It's uncomfortable like an artist showing his first piece in public.

"She's fucking hot!"

"You should've seen her shaking on the ground."

Eve giggles.

"Babe, you need to get her down."

I slowly bring down her now pale body. It's cold to the touch and the heavy blood has dried on her skin.

Once I lower Brooklyn's flaccid body after unlatching her from the shower, Eve is already waiting for me with several large black trash bags.

She's in charge and on the same page as me, "put her in the bathtub, we need to cut up her body in sections".

I toss her body in the same bathtub and walk back to the room to retrieve the saw.

She takes it from my hand and stands square over the dead body. Pointing the end of the shovel down, she stabs it directly into Brooklyn's upper arm. Eve is laughing. She's like a girl at the fair, hitting her target for a prize.

She's accurate because the arm is easily severed with three hits. She does the same process with the other arm while stepping over Brooklyn, and placing her foot on the soap holder inside the shower wall. She's bent over and her spine is showing. She does it this time in two hits, spiking the shovel through the bone and into the ceramic tub. A loud crunch echoes into the halls.

She hands me the shovel saw combo out of breath, "It's your turn. Cut off her thick legs".

I'll do anything Eve tells me to do. Her investment in my extracurricular activity is fascinating.

Brooklyn's body has been divided into five parts. Her torso is large and the head needs to be removed.

Eve takes the knife still placed inside the tub, coated with Brooklyn's red paint, and washes it off in the sink.

"I want the head." She coldly says without looking at me.

By grabbing the cover still over Brooklyn's face she begins digging the knife into the throat. A few squirts of blood trickle out and through she pillow sheet. She moves her knife up and down, sawing around the spine. By holding the knife handle with one hand she uses her other as a mallet to dislocate the head from the spinal column.

"Get me the bags," She orders me.

I open the first bag wide and she tosses in the heavy head. We pack our belongings like a family going on vacation. The ends are double knotted and enclosed tight with the duct tape.

"Go get the car and park it backwards in the driveway."

Again I do as I'm told, and when I reverse the car in I see Eve waiting for me with a bag in each hand. We load up the trunk and she has my duffel bag on her lap once jumping into the passenger seat.

"I poured the rest of the vinegar all over the bathroom, especially in the tub."

"How did you learn to do all that?" I can't help but ask.

"Same way you probably learned to kill women."

"Trial and error?" I smile at her, for what I think is the first time in my life.

We both laugh on the way to an abandoned warehouse I've visited multiple times. It's so vacant that not even homeless people gather around. No one else will need to be killed tonight.

#

Eve and I were surging with so much adrenaline after burying the body parts through an opening in the warehouse floor. The hole was filled with construction debris and covered with a large metal sheet.

I saw her shaking on the way back to the car. I haven't been able to catch my breath.

We haven't showered yet, and both our hands are stained red with the first degree of what we've committed. Her nails are a pretty shade of pink.

We pull into a park that is still empty this early in the morning. We make out in the backseat for what feels like both a paucity in time and an eternity.

I finger her with two, and then three fingers. The dry blood on my hands mixed with her grool, makes for the wettest pussy. Her moaning in my face is the most enchanting music I've ever heard. She's sucking on my upper lip while I finger fuck her insides.

She rides me cowgirl. Because I just came several hours ago, I last longer than I ever have. She grinds on me long enough that we're both sweating. The windows of my small car are covered in steam.

While we're both climaxing she whispers in my ear, "How does it feel to make two girls cum in one day?".

I don't respond with words, but I grab her hips to move them back and forth on top of me. She's rubbing her clit against my pelvic bone. She moans while I ejaculate into a more beautiful girl than the last. But instead of my victim, she's my inspiration. My muse and my guide. My everything.

Once we're done and clean up after ourselves, we take a walk around the park. I go back to the car and grab a pill from the glovebox. This is too good to ruin with The Board running shit.

We're holding hands and talking about the different severities of heinous crimes we could exact on innocent people. Our roles and how to get away with it each time.

If this is love then it's more than I could have ever understood. It's a puzzle which has been deciphered. Unraveled before me with me at the core. If this is potentially what people talk about when a soul has met its match, then I want to do this forever. I want to do this every week.

#

We've been walking for hours. We've left the confines of the park, and entered unfamiliar spaces. We don't want the moment to end.

Our conversation becomes more absorbing with every subsequent minute. I've looked into her eyes over a hundred times. I've checked out her body from as many angles as I conceivably can with our clothes on.

Our feet have led us into a dark neighborhood with criminals on every corner. Our morning stroll has called attention to us from a house with dangerous looking men perched on the front porch and sitting on the stoop.

“You motherfuckers lost!?!?”, a drug dealer among many shouts at my girl and me.

She leans into me while we’re approaching the front of their property.

“You should teach him a lesson for me. I’ll be ready to run.”

I’m looking for a flaw in her statement. I know that most of these men are armed. But a surprise attack is effective only if an escape is mapped out. And she looks like she’s faster than me, so I’m not worried for my safety, or hers.

“Hey cuz! Let me talk to your bitch!!” they all start laughing and calling for Eve. “Bring that skank over here!”

My right hand starts trembling and I have to put it in my pocket to hide what I’m thinking.

She whispers without moving her mouth and keeping her eyes fixed forward.

“Kill that one. He’s the pack leader.” Once again she’s not wrong.

We’re stopped at the front. I try to act like a druggy. I walk toward them in long strides and I’m wobbly.

“Do you have pills? I need a fix.”

“Ohhh shit! He’s a customer!” they cheer and laugh at me.

Once he’s within my reach I lunge forward and with both thumbs I run them through his eyes. I aim for the pupil. I gouge the bullseye to lacerate his cornea in one swift movement.

“AAAHHHHHH WHAT THE FU…!!!” He screeches while blood pours down his cheeks.

His fellow beasts start howling in unity at my attack. One tries to grab me. I sprint off the porch, and jump over a small fence. I make it over three front yards before I meet with Eve on the same street.

We hear gunshots and bullets ricocheting the concrete around us.

Eve is laughing hysterically while darting at full speed. She's a wonder.

I take a peek at her broad smile mid-gallop. She's breathtaking. How, when, why did I get so lucky?

#

We stop at a fast food chain to get a bite to eat. All this murdering and blinding peeps really works up an appetite.

We're looking at the menu board with more meals than I know what to do with. She asks me what I want, and I tell her I'm still thinking.

"What do you want to eat?" I return the question.

"I don't know. I don't see anything I like."

"This was your idea. You picked the place."

"I know but I'm not even that hungry."

"You're the one that said we should eat…"

"Hey, don't get snarky with me. I could tell you were famished after the night you've had." She nudges my arm with her arm.

"I have food at my place, but you said you had enough money to pay for this."

"I do, and it was a suggestion. Don't go getting sensitive with me!"

"I'm not fucking sensitive. I'm waiting on you."

"Why are you being mean to me right now!" She's starting to yell.

"Calm the fuck down. People are starting to stare at us." I grab her by the arm.

"Ryder, trust me I can make a fucking scene, asshole! Don't test me!"

"Eve! We need to leave." I pull her out the door while families are watching our every move.

But she keeps yelling, "You ever treat me like that again, I fucking swear to god, Ryder!!!".

She's punching the hood of my car, and I worry that she'll break her hand.

"Please calm the fuck down! Look I'm sorry!" I don't think I've ever apologized for anything in my life.

Eve is stopped in her tracks standing straight, staring right at me.

She's wearing small shorts and flip flops. Her belly button is showing and her long brown hair is in a messy bun. I don't think I've ever seen a more terrifying vision.

I don't know how to interpret her position, but I'm perpetually turned on by her face. By the things she says to me.

She finally gets in the car. And slams the door to make sure I'm aware of what she's feeling.

"Where are we heading?" I ask her once we've sat in front of the fast food place for an unreasonable amount of time.

"I want to see where you live." She urges.

"You're not ready."

"You're not ready to show me." Her god damn counters.

"Fuck it, let's go." I concede.

Ecstasy salivating at the mouth
Euphoria rubbing away all concern.

Chapter 19

Shared Psychosis

It's in the middle of the afternoon. We've skipped breakfast and lunch.

Against my reluctance I show Eve the inside of my trailer home.

She walks in slowly. To take it all in.

I lock the door behind her.

She's made it in this far so there won't be any premature departure or retreat.

She walks around the limited floorplan. From my arm's length living room, to my makeshift kitchen counter, to the hall that takes two steps to enter a bedroom mostly comprised of a queen sized mattress.

Eve runs her hand against the walls of the living room down to the halls. She's trying to decipher my black inscriptions inked on all of the walls from floor to ceiling. My compass will never make sense to her, but she devotes attention to every symbol no less.

She looks inside the crimson stained bathroom and back at me, with that infamous smile.

"You really like doing your work in bathrooms don't you."

I pull up my sleeve to show her the scar on my forearm.

"I tried to stitch this. But fucked it up."

She walks over to where I'm standing, in the hall, and grabs my arm like Lizbeth did that one time.

She shows concern, "Holy shit balls, what did you do to yourself?!".

Although I can't tell if it's genuine or feigned, I enjoy it.

She moves past me and stands over the La-Z-Boy recliner, squared like she did before hacking off Brooklyn's limbs.

She picks up my hardened cum rag, "Is this where you, umm, jack off?".

I don't know what to say. I never considered she would find the most intimate places where I conduct myself and question me about it.

"Uh, ya, yeah" I struggle to say it.

She smells it and I'm about to pass out from the influx of self-consciousness into my face. I can sense the heat effusing from my pores. But I can't look away. And fortunately she doesn't hold on to it too long.

"Have you ever masturbated thinking about me?" there are those eyes, soul sucking me with more pressure than her tongue.

I stare right back without a blink, "More times than I can count."

She looks away and starts rummaging through my things.

"Make me food. I'm hungry." She read my mind.

Anything to change the subject. To move on to the next line.

I prepare her my best gourmet dish of pan-fried albacore over buttered soba noodles with ketchup glace. She and I scarf it down. And shower immediately after. We needed to wash the sin off of us. We airdry naked with nothing clean to dry ourselves with.

We crash immediately once we're done with food consumption. Falling asleep on my bare bed. With no heat or blanket for covering, I hold her to keep her warm. Her arms are covered by my arms, and her two legs are covered by my large leg.

I've never been held or have held another. Our bodies fit together like two puzzle pieces from different jigsaws. Irregular and yet counterparts compatible to each other, without having to force it.

We're interlocked until a greater force can separate what we are, bonded.

This shit is powerful. Our lives are chaotically intertwined like a mosaic of maroon and ebony blended without dividing lines.

#

We wake up an entire 18 hours later.

Or at least I did. I opened my eyes to the absence of her warm body under mine.

I know she's still in my home because I can hear clatter. Eve is moving stuff around and humming some old Western tune.

Walking out of my small room, standing by the bathroom door, I see everything has been picked up. Things are arranged in an appealing fashion. My hotplate is no longer bent. My radio has been put together, turned on, and situated in a better place. I'm scanning the small trailer for my cum rag and blood soaked towel, but they're nowhere to be found.

"We need to get you new towels." Somehow she's reading my thoughts.

"You didn't have to do any of this." I'm not annoyed, I'm more surprised.

"No man of mine is going to live in a pigsty." She corrects me while still cleaning.

"You should make this your place as well." I pitch a wild idea.

"I don't want to return to my grandmother's. She weakens me." She's speaking in code again, but if it means she'll remain I'll allow it.

What did I do to deserve this? Are the people that I've killed so deserving of their deaths that I'm being rewarded? Where did she come from, where did I go wrong to be sent someone as benevolent as she is?

I walk over to her and turn her toward me. I can't help myself but deliver a long kiss. She jumps on me. I'm holding her under her firm ass while she dry humps my pelvis.

Eve is thrown on the recliner sofa.

She squeaks while laughing out loudly, "Ah you motherfucker!"

I get on my knees.

Her short shorts are pulled off. She doesn't wear any panties.

Grabbing her behind the legs, I pull her closer to me. She looks uncomfortable, with her head bent forward and her chin on her chest. But at least her pussy is facing up and easier to eat.

I'm holding her legs wide, against the armrests on each side. She's flexible.

I first start kissing around her outer lips. They're small and somewhat a darker color than her skin. I bite her inner thighs. I leave teeth marks right where her inner legs and groin meet.

She's already moaning.

Just how I kissed her face, I kiss her pussy. Between her inner lips, I move my puckered mouth left and right, while pushing my face forward against her accumulation of skin. I make way for my tongue but not before I nudge her clit three times with the tip of my nose.

I want, I need to taste the inside of her. I stick my tongue as far deep as I can. It's outstretched into her vagina. I move it around in a circle motion, clockwise so that every drop of her organ is tasted on every inch of my tongue. I remove it all the way out and insert it all the way in again, all the way out, and all the way in. And point it up toward the inside of her clit. To flick it back out.

Her vulva is dripping now, puddling under her ass.

Her inner labia are a bright pink. The right one is sucked. The left inner lip is put in my mouth and moved around with my saliva, then sucked dry. I do it again to the right inner lip.

Her entire vulva is glimmering in the bright room. Her clit is protruding out past its hood.

She begs me, "suck my clit, please suck my clit."

I slowly, with the very end of my wet tongue, start to move it over her clitoral hood. It's being rotated counterclockwise.

Eve is rocking her hips.

My tongue is slowly placing more pressure over her clitoris, shifting it around in circles.

I let go and spit on it.

When I return to her perfect looking pussy, I place my upper lip right above her hood. My lower lip is pressed right above her vagina hole. And I slowly start to suck, increasing the pressure within my mouth. I'm pulling in inner labia into my mouth and moving her clitoral hood up with my upper lip.

When I can feel her pulsating clitoris against my tongue, I start swiping it with the entire width of my moist appendage left and right. My tongue is pushing as hard as it can, while sliding the hole at the center of her clitoris from the left side of my tongue all the way across to the right side. Back again to the left and slowly to the right, left and then right.

Now faster, left, right, left, and right.

I reposition my lips to get a better grip and suck in as hard as I can. My tongue glides across her clitoris rapidly now. To the left, and to the right. Left, Right, Left, Right, Left, Right.

Two fingers are slipped inside and pushed against the ridges of her internal clit. In unison with the metronome movement of my mouth, my fingers are rubbing left and right as well, but even faster than my tongue.

"OH MY FUCKING GOD! DON'T STOP"

Saliva and cum are trickling down my chin and pooling on the cushion beneath.

"FUCK! FUCK! FUCK!"

I flick my two fingers out, against the roof of her vagina, and stick them back in. I rub the upper portion of her vaginal opening again and again, while not missing a beat with my tongue.

She's about to cum.

My face is shaking aggressively to the left and right, and finally she squirts in my mouth. Water is spraying out of her urethra but I don't stop rubbing it from side to side. My fingers have been pushed out of her vagina, so I rub the inner labia with the same two fingers.

"AAAHHHH AHH AHH, MY GOD!"

She's pushing my head into her crotch while squirting all over me. She's showering me with her orgasm.

She's shaking. Her legs are vibrating and stiff. She hasn't stopped gyrating her hips and grinding them on my face.

I separate myself from her crotch and rub her legs all the way up to her ribs. Her nipples are hardened and pinched with both my thumbs and pointer fingers.

I give her the biggest kiss, so that she can taste what I taste. Her flavor is the sweetest nectar and shouldn't be wasted.

#

We play with each other's bodies for hours. Long into the night.

I haven't taken my medications in two days.

I crash around 1 am, after ejaculating twice. Eve is lying next to me, but not cuddling up to me this time. I can hear her masturbating while I sleep. In the brief moments that I toss or turn, the bed is moving as she's sighing delicately.

And in the morning when I wake up she's rummaging again through my things.

"What are you doing?" I ask her while I put on my clothes and regain my bearings.

"I'm looking for a tool. To fix your air conditioner."

"It doesn't need to be fixed."

"Yea it does, Ryder! It's fucking freezing in here!"

"Why are you yelling? I didn't ask you to do anything."

We told you she wasn't right for you, my lovely. Mrs. Bathory speaks.

Where the fuck did she come from?

"If I'm going to stay here, we need to get some things in order! I can't live like this!" Eve is looking toward me, but past me.

This one is as crazy as a runover cat! Fucking Farmer John is back.

"You're pissed off that you're here?" I need to clear this up with her.

"I love you, but you live like an animal, Ryder." She just admitted to loving me.

"I…I…like the way I live." I can't reciprocate her emotion.

I don't feel that shit. Or maybe I don't know how to feel that.

"Real fucking nice! I knew you were just using me. You just needed me to get you out of trouble!!" She's screaming at the top of her lungs.

"I never used you once!"

She's a scarlet, son. You don't trust a scarlet with your life. Professor Marks just showed up.

The Board is present again. Fuck! It's because I haven't taken my medications. And I can't go looking for them right now because Eve is in my face, albeit her forehead is the height of my chin.

"Ryder, you called me to help you get rid of her body! You fucking waited for me at college! You planned all of this!!!" I didn't know her small body could produce such a loud voice.

We're at risk of the neighbors hearing our entire argument. Because I can clearly hear it when they fight like this.

"I love that you were down to help me with the body. I love that you're into the shit that I'm into!"

"Oh now you can say the L word! You're such a dick!!!"

She isn't going to calm down. You need to calm this whore down, the only way you know how, dearest. Mrs. Bathory is the last voice I need right now.

"I bet you're planning to kill me just like you killed Brooklyn!!!" She's blaring out our secrets with no care of who's walking outside or nearby.

"Eve, please! Calm the fuck down!!"

Look at him beggin' like a mutt with his tail between his legs!

She's starting to pace up and down my trailer home. From the end of the hallway into the room and back to me in front of the mini kitchen.

She picks up a steak knife. And waves it in my face with the pointed edge inches from my skin.

"You've been plotting to find me before killing that girl. Which means you've been scheming to lock me here, haven't you!"

Someone like her is delusional. She needs to be at a psychiatric facility. Mr. Solomon isn't helping.

"Put that fucking knife down." I command her before I think of the worst.

"This knife is my protection against you."

She's going to kill you, my lovely. You need to kill her first.

"No, she's not!" I hold my head as it starts to hurt.

"Who the fuck are you talking to??"

"You don't need to be protected against me. You can leave whenever the fuck you'd like." I try to talk calm but this is too much.

She's snarling. She has a look in her eyes like a caged animal.

"You're fucking crazy. Get the fuck away from me." She threatens me while getting closer with the knife.

If one believes they're more ill than others, then that's the sign of true insanity.

"She's not insane! She's scared!" I yell at The Board to leave us in peace.

"See I might be manic but you're a fucking maniac!" I'm not registering what she's trying to tell me.

The only door of this plastic trailer is flung open and I stand next to it.

"You can leave, baby. I'm not keeping you here." I show her both of my palms.

"You're such a fucking manipulator!!!" She reacts.

"I just want to make you happy." I try my best to reason with her, to be honest to her.

"Yea you fucking wish. You're a basket case."

Eve grabs her sandals and storms out. She throws the knife at me and misses my head by a foot.

We warned you that she was disturbed. Professor Marks is providing his useless retrospect.

What the fuck just happened? Where did I just fuck up?

Somehow, I'm worried for Eve.

I need to fix this.

A mother's love is a mother's bond.
But when mother is gone, she breaks her son.

Chapter 20

Oedipus Complex

I don't know where to go. I haven't the slightest clue of what to do.

Eve hasn't called. She hasn't come back to our home.

I've sat in the same chair where I ate her out. Not moving a muscle. I'm catatonic. Aware that I have no physical activity, nor desire to activate my body.

But I haven't stopped arguing with the voices in my head.

You're better off without her, my beloved.

"Anything is better than being here, bitch. She made this place bearable."

She just ain't what ya need.

"You have no fucking idea what it is I need, you hick."

Right before I fall into a deep state of trance where they drown me, a loud knock is blown on my door.

I look out the window on the side of the trailer. It's two large men, not in any formal drab. They're wearing button down shirts with their sleeves rolled up.

It's finally happening, they're here for me. I've been found.

I open it slowly, and as I'm looking down at the handle, I remember I'm only in my boxers. Eve and I were walking around the place naked for most of the time.

"Ryder Strickland?" The one who's standing closer asks.

"That…is me."

"Sir, we're from Newburgh State Hospital, in Cleveland. My name is Mr. Erickson and this is Mr. Addams."

Fancy that lad, last time you heard, your mother was locked up in Cleveland. Professor Marks refreshes my recollection.

"I don't know anyone in Cleveland. What do you all want?"

"Sir, your mother, Aileen Strickland, is a long term resident at our facility and…" The man standing closest to me explains.

The other one interrupts him, "She was involved in an attack."

"Of course (nodding my head). What kind of fucking attack?"

"Unfortunately she attacked another resident. She was pushed off and fell down the stairs, causing an internal brain bleed with her spine fractured. Right now she's in critical care." The main one takes the lead again.

"Sounds like she lost."

Your mother has always been the instigator. Mr. Solomon reminds me.

"Son, we need…"

"Sir, I ain't nobody's son."

I start closing my door, but I'm blocked when the lead gets on my steps and puts his foot down.

"Ryder. She's asking for you to be there. We don't think she's going to make it."

"Why do you give a fuck?"

The other behind him talks out of turn again, "Aileen has been an important pillar at our facility".

"A pillar?"

"Yes sir, for over five years."

"She's been the one to help new women adjust to the institute. She's earned our care and respect."

"That's some funny shit." I smile for the second time in my life.

Rarely am I confronted with true irony in real life. Where an afflicted individual who has burned everyone near and dear to her, is now beloved because she's found some façade of mentorship. That bitch shouldn't be anywhere near susceptible women.

"Ryder, the hospital is almost 3 hours away. We wouldn't have driven all the way here if it wasn't life and death."

I do know that Mother was transferred out of a local psychiatric facility to a more intensive one. Something about being too volatile or repeated attempts to escape.

She don't want you, you know that. So don't waste yer motherfuckin' breath!

"What exactly do you all want from me? There isn't anything that I can do if she's about to die."

"Aileen is asking for you, son. Would you come by and sit with her? It's her last and only wish." The main man takes off his sunglasses while making his thoughtful request.

"I volunteer at the fire station. I've got to be back this afternoon."

You know all too well that the fire department isn't in need of your services. The professor offers no useful insight.

"That's all we're asking of you."

If Eve decides to come home or call me back then I want to be in the vicinity to receive her.

#

Mother was never a warm parental figure. Any form of palpable energy was felt during our heated exchanges. So to expect anything else from her is out of the ordinary. It's as foreign to her and I's connection, as unnatural, as a shark raising her young.

I don't join the men in their car. I don't fucking trust anyone or anything.

Are you sure this is in your best interest? Mr. Solomon poses a philosophical question.

My interest is in making problems go away. And if this is the ticket to getting rid of Mother for good then I'll take it.

It's already been a long car ride. I've been driving for about two hours on half a tank. The fellas chipped in about ten dollars for fuel.

I feel responsible for Mother and guilty at the same time, since I didn't tell Eve I was leaving. Though I doubt she would have answered me calling.

My mind is racing with the possible outcomes of all of this. That I'll be attacked once again. Or that she'll find a way to escape me without thought of what I'm supposed to do once she leaves. Maybe she's going to try to rebuild the negligible blood relationship her and I have.

But as the men who are now enchanted by her are showing that impossible things are possible to shift, I'm expecting the awkward exchange with her. I'm trying to find words to use and ways of saying phrases that emphasize the slightest form of caring.

If the quality of a mother and child's relationship is measured in the child's relationship with his women, then I can only assume one would think that my torture of the female gender is indicative of a sadistic attachment. She never showed concern for the shit that I endured, but more on how to inflict more pain during the shit I was living through.

I've arrived at the huge facility. I was following the gentleman in their newer sedan this entire trip.

This here is as bad an idea as a monkey fuckin' a football. Country ass John tries to quip.

"If she does her old song and dance then I'm leaving." I tell The Board while getting out of the vehicle.

The two representatives are looking at me.

#

They walk me through the side door of the immense hospital. They show security their badges and I'm escorted through the metal screen.

Hallway after hallway, much longer ones than Eloise. I'm taken on enough twists and turns to make my head spin.

At the end of a dark enough corridor on some second or third floor, is her brightly lit room.

They point at it without entering before me.

"She's in there. You can stay as long you need."

#

I stand at the threshold of her infirmary room. I can see her feet outside of the sheets.

I slowly walk over to Mother.

Her eyes are opened and looking vacantly at the ceiling.

"Mother."

She turns her wrinkled face to her right. Her green dots are staring into my brown eyes.

She's expressionless.

Don't trust this bitch. Bathory coldly recites.

"What makes you think I want you here?", is the first thing she utters, barely audible with her raspy voice.

I done told you she was foolin' ya!

Honestly you can't say you're surprised, my dear.

“They…, the two men…came and got me. That you fucking asked for me.”

“I asked for a fucking soda pop. Not my worthless son.” She looks away while saying this.

I turn to walk away. I’m in no mood to deal with her bullshit.

This is all a game to her. She’s always pulled these sorts of stunts. To get a rise out of me or to find a way to make me ruin everything.

Right when I reach the door, she speaks up one last time.

“Aren’t you going to tell me that you’re proud of me?”

“For what?”, I speak louder than her without turning around.

“For becoming someone to these people. Better than you’ll ever be able to say for yourself.”

One’s negative view of their self has nothing to do with you. Solomon’s right.

“That’s why you attacked another woman like you. You must feel pretty good for being the abuser like the old you.” I walk back toward her.

“You wouldn’t know abuse if it took a shit in your mouth. Guess what honey, I do.”

Hot damn! She’s a nasty bitch! Farmer John ain’t wrong.

“You must be happy with how you ended up then.” I talk lower.

“You think I don’t know you, Ryder. You think I don’t know what you’ve been up to?”

She don’t know her ass from her elbow.

“You don’t know your arthritic ass from your pimpled elbow.” That wasn’t my best work.

I stand over her bed for one last time. To lean into her and whisper right above her head.

“If you ever contact me again, by phone or by sending your messenger men, I’m going to find everything you give a fuck about and burn it to the ground. Don’t test me, Mother.”

She whispers right back, “There’s not a thing in this world I give a fuck about. Including you, Ry”.

I walk away before choking her out. I won’t be put away for manslaughter, no less on my own mother.

She doesn’t care about you like we do, Ryder. Mrs. Bathory chimes in on the most inopportune time.

Before leaving this forsaken hospital, where Aileen has cast her spells, the two pliant men stop me in the hall.

“Ryder, we’d like to speak with you.”

You should’ve kept your cool. They heard everything. Mrs. Bathory distresses me.

They’ll commence an investigation on you with just one phone call. Professor Marks menaces.

“About what.” I try to stare them down but it doesn’t seem to work on their dreary eyes.

“Aileen was supposed to have a hearing next week. But she…(sighs) started this attack.”

“We watched it multiple times on camera video footage. And we can’t make sense why.”

“I’ll never understand that woman. I doubt you all ever will.”

"The thing is…we haven't been fully honest with you." Mr. Addams looks down while he says it.

Mr. Erickson places his hand on his chest, "I'm her therapist and this is her case worker".

You know far too well that woman should never be released. Professor Marks forewarns.

You shouldn't trust these fellas as far as you can throw em'! Farmer John has a point.

"Why was she going to get released?" I confirm the mistake the system was about to commit.

"Conditionally." Mr. Addams elucidates.

"To a half-way house." Mr. Erickson adds.

"But what's makes you all believe she's ready to rejoin society?"

One could argue you're not right for society. Mr. Solomon isn't wrong.

"The way she's helped these women, her commitment to seeing them acclimate and thrive in this…difficult circumstance was, is awe-inspiring." Mr. Erickson almost has tears in his eyes.

"So let her keep doing it. I don't want anything to do with her." I try to remove myself from the equation.

"If you could speak at the hearing about what she was like before she committed the murder, then that'll strengthen our argument that she's been reformed. Which is made obvious by the good work she's done here for the past 5 years." Mr. Addams expounds on their true purpose.

"Without any incident like the one she's in since being admitted." Mr. Erickson tacks on.

"If she makes it, you want me to describe, in detail, the kind of woman…the kind of mother she was before she was supposed to be put away for good? For kidnapping and torture?" I verify the extent that they need me to be honest.

Cause the honest truth is as fucked up as fucked up gets. The redneck couldn't be more right.

Mr. Erickson is talking with his hands, "We're using the clinical basis of Battered Women's Syndrome to defend her actions. That she has a history of trauma and psychosis, and that her partner put so much abuse on her, she eventually cracked. But she's been rehabilitated with therapy and medications."

"If, and when, she makes it, we hope that the current altercation won't impact the court's decision. But that'll be out of our hands."

"You fucking guys, with your degrees, have more hope than I'll ever hold for her. But sure, I'll tell the court exactly what kind of woman she was prior to being locked up. If she makes it."

You should tell them precisely what she did to you all those years. Mrs. Bathory and I agree on that.

The court will be informed of Mother's depraved nature. That their beloved Aileen has a side to her that is not only inhuman, but that she's capable of being vindictive.

Especially during her psychotic states. Professor Marks remembers.

I plan on showing them the scars on my body. And the stories behind each.

I'll recount the things she's said to me. The things she believes.

What her and I went through. And how I was the object of her displaced anger.

The target of her resentment.

Her reflection of hatred.

Always ready for a fire. Too steady to expire.

Chapter 21

He's Damned If I Do, He's Damned If I Don't

After returning to my unhappy home, it was a long night. I was able to get some light sleep, filled with heated debate from The Board.

The voices reprimanded me for the situation with Eve. They all gave their two cents on how to handle the hearing. They appealed for me to take out my frustrations on an innocent woman. Mrs. Bathory wants me to burn down a house filled with people.

It's now 7 am, and I don't have much to do without Eve, school, or the fire department. Idle hands are making the devil come out of me.

Someone should be punished for my state of affairs. Nothing eases the mind like beating the fat out of someone's body. Just as the dark thoughts of finding my next victim are intruding into my brain, my phone vibrates.

It's the fire station.

Of course I pick up immediately, expecting news that I'm under arrest and that I should present myself at the nearest police station.

It's the Chief, "Ryder, how are you son?"

"I'm good, Chief. How can I help you?"

"Well I have some news about the investigation."

I'm not sure if he's expecting me to say something about it or to admit to anything, but a long pause was present between us.

He finally speaks again, "We've been carrying out an internal investigation, and we have some additional questions".

Don't you answer anything he has to say. Mrs. Bathory

"Sure, what sort of questions?" I'm feeling confident.

"Well…could you come in today to clear up a few things?" The Chief asks but it sounds like an order.

"I can't today sir, I have a college class and an appointment with my psychiatrist."

That was as stupid as dumb gets! Farmer John tries to shame me.

Do you not suppose that they'll look into you're psychiatrist's office?! Professor Marks is irate.

I highly doubt that the fire marshal analyzing the fire and the homicide detective looking into the murder will ever connect.

"Son, this takes precedence over anything else you've got going on."

"I understand sir. But if I miss today's appointment I won't get a refill of my medication and I'm all out."

"Fine. Then make it in first thing tomorrow morning. Copy?"

"Roger, sir."

#

I don't have college nor any doctor's appointment today.

I'm trying to buy myself time. I don't feel like going in to answer any questions. Because the last thing my mind is focused on is the pointless investigation.

I've left the trailer home and I'm on the prowl.

It's some time in the early afternoon.

The Board has convinced me to find a potential victim. Someone unknown to us, never before seen.

You should identify a female victim of random selection. Mr. Solomon advises.

A nobody! Farmer John assists.

We've been driving around for what seems like three hours. In and out of residential neighborhoods. Through alleys and streets known to be frequented by prostitutes. Around clubs and bars where women are out having a ball.

#

We've pulled into a rundown community. Some urban shithole similar to mine. It's not a trailer park, but small homes that aren't well kempt. My windows are down to get a better view of these austere surroundings.

There aren't any people out socializing like the darker communities. But I've seen a few druggies walking around more delirious than the residents at Eloise Hospital.

A pretty woman has just got off the bus at the end of the street. She's walking toward me, and I've just passed her.

I don't have anywhere to U-turn so I turn right on the next street. I'll circle back to watch where she's heading. Where she ends up.

On my second right, driving in the parallel direction as her, smoke is being pushed out of a worn down house. It's ragged and falling apart. The smoke is dark and fuming a smell of ammonia.

I pull over to watch the action.

The smoke increases in volume and small flames begin to fan out of one of the windows.

A loud pop, a small explosion blows out the windows from where the smoke began. A medium size fire starts to rage on the right side of the house, where the front door is held.

Well isn't this a delectable coincidence, isn't it lovely? Mrs. Bathory excites.

She isn't wrong but I'm interested to see how this plays out. It would seem that people are inside, yet I haven't heard any screaming.

You could be startin' yer own screamin' with that gal down the street. Farmer John prefers rape over fire.

"The bitch from the bus stop is going to have to wait."

The fire is now loud. Within seconds, a raging orange and yellow are fueling out of what looks like the kitchen.

There's a child's bicycle in the front yard and clothes scattered about.

This is a meth house and the detonation has just occurred. The people inside are probably a small family, but within seconds of being exterminated by their own vices.

If you save them then the Chief is forced to view you in a brighter light. Professor Marks encourages me to act.

Nothing says innocent more than a hero doing what's right. Mrs. Bathory is also onboard.

I push my small vehicle over to the side and turn it off after touching the curb.

I put on my only other hoodie that I own, a grey sweater. I pour water over my head and arms in expectation of walking through some high temperature heat.

I run over to the side where there's less smoke and hopefully no blaze. The window is already cracked so an elbow to the center is sufficient to shatter the glass. I crawl through but I can barely see through the pitch black haze or breathe with the smell of cat urine filling my chest.

A little child is weeping in one room and a grown man's voice is yelling from an open bathroom right next to it.

"HELLLLPPP!!! We're stuck in here!!!" He calls for help.

I do the logical thing and open the door of the bedroom where the child is screeching his little heart away. In the far corner near the closet is a mother holding her small child. Their heads are face down. They're shaking in this hot house, but out of pure fear.

Both sets of eyes look anxiously at me. They're whimpering and begging for someone, like me, to bail them out of this mess they've been put in.

I close the door. My arm is covering my nose.

The bathroom next door is cracked open. The father figure hasn't stopped yelling. I kick it violently open. The man bounces back from the swift movement.

"My wife and kid! They're somewhere in here! Please!"

A ceiling support collapses behind me, barely missing my back. An eruption of dust and more black fog is released simultaneously. The internal heat from an observable swelling in flames is growing to an intolerable degree.

The four of us are cooking alive in this drug den. My sweater and pants are drenched in sweat from my skin. This family will be terminated within minutes from being roasted alive.

The decision to save them is within my reach. I've decided that I can grab them and make it to safety outside but just once and only one time. With the suffocating level of danger inside rising, I won't be able to return for a second rescue. This is a now or never, do or die type of scenario.

I walk through the open door. I'm basically making my way through by short term memory. I'm stepping in slowly as to not trip over anything on the floor.

I grab a body sitting in the fetal position in a dirty corner. It's shaking. I throw it over my shoulders in a fireman carry technique.

I could grab a second body and toss it over on my other shoulder. These people looked malnourished enough to not be that heavy for me. But only one body will do.

The man on my back is coughing up his little lung. He's now crying uncontrollably. He's pathetic, fucking useless.

He's close to havin' a dying duck fit! Farmer John laughs as he says it.

The choice I had between picking him or the remainder of his small family, was simple. Save the woman and child or save the drug cooking man of the house.

I choose the father. He'll forever be scarred from this. The melted blood of his insignificant family will forever be stained on his wife-beater shirt.

I trod with him outside and plunk him on a brown spot in the yard. He's hacking and heaving, rolling around getting his thin cooking attire all muddy.

I kneel down in front of him, down on one knee. I want to watch his facial expression when the news hits.

He's on all fours trying his overstimulated best to regain an appearance of composure. He's drooling on himself, snot bubbles are popping out of his nostrils. Tears are runneling down his stupid face.

"Whe…whe…where's my family?!" he hollers.

Won't he be gobsmacked about the end to his fairytale? Professor Marks is tickled about the current scene unfolding.

He's looking around warringly without being able to clearly see. Shaking his head to the left, right, and straight ahead.

"Where did they…Did you…get my family?"

I'm watching his eyes closely. Not saying a fucking word, nor giving him any sign of emotion. The juncture where his life ends and the nightmare begins is happening right before me.

I'm salivating at what I'm witnessing.

"Please, please…tell me (cough)… where's my family!?" he's yanking on my sweatshirt hysterically.

The sirens of a nearby firetruck are becoming higher in frequency as they're nearing. A local engine must be responding and it'll be here any moment.

They'll soon thank you, dearest. Mrs. Bathory prepares me.

The team is now in sight.

"WHERE THE FUCK IS MY FAMILY, MAN!?!?!?"

A fascinating choice of words. Professor Marks proclaims.

He's starting to get the message and the terror in his eyes begins to surface. The house is in full tilt, crackling and hissing while walls are toppling over.

The fire engine pulls in and five men jump out. Like a well-choreographed ensemble they all carry out their assignments with few words. The lead, likely a lieutenant, walks right at us.

"Were you two in the house when the fire began?"

I stand up and reach out to shake his hand, "This man was in the home, My name is Ryder, I'm a volunteer at Engine 33. I was only able to get him, but I'm not sure if there are any more".

"Looks like you saved his life, Ryder. Job well done, we'll take it from here." He squeezes my hand with intensity.

Told you, dearest.

I make sure to stay to watch that no other bodies are pulled from the scorching home. The hose takes some time to lessen the blaze. What's left is a charred structure with a few beams barely still in place.

The man is a blubbering mess. His screams are the type that are hard to forget.

He's calling out their names persistently, "MONICA…!!! HALEY…!!! MONICA…!!! HALEY…!!!".

He'll never stop suffering. Because of my action and equal inaction, the consequence of his living style will forever traumatize him.

You've proven yourself today young man. Mr. Solomon congratulates.

Job well done, old chap. Professor Marks toasts my name.

Thataboy! Farmer John is delighted.

Mrs. Bathory isn't left out, *We knew you could fix this*.

My face will forever be engrained in memory of his family dying. I'm the most important person in his life, from here on out.

I'm the reaper of everything he loves. Yet the savior of what he'll have to face, his worthless life.

Better to have loved, than not love a slut.
But to have been loved with lust is embrace disguised as loss.

Chapter 22

Return of the Knight

The drive home, this time, is a celebratory one. It's late into the evening. I don't think I've been this elated in quite a while.

In a singular deed I've changed not only my life, but the course, albeit short ones, of three others.

Eve would be so proud of me.

#

I haven't been this invigorated since killing Brooklyn. I can't wait for the Chief to hear about this. I'm close to contacting him myself so that he can hear it from me.

Don't ya go putting' the cart before the horse. Farmer John prompts more patience.

I theorize that jacking off would vent some much needed steam. Thinking of the man's woman, of her eyes in need are really doing it. I'm envisioning fucking her brains out in the middle of the house as it collapses. I'm stroking myself with two hands while thinking of pounding her sweaty pussy as her partner in crime cowers in the smoke-filled bathroom. Imagining myself cumming in her pussy and leaving her on the floor shaking right before the house is set to uncontrollable flames makes my testes release everything I've built up inside me. Having her life in my literal hands within a sexual fire is a turn on I haven't yet become familiarized with.

Right after my ejaculate has spewed on my thighs, as I'm wiping the sperm cells with a new towel that Eve brought for me, the door of my humble home is being thumped upon.

Three loud raps, quickly in succession.

That was quick for Chief Crassus to hear the story of my altruism. He's come here, personally, to salute me.

You better finally thank us after all this. Mrs. Bathory prefaces the next scene.

I open it slowly, to build the tension within my narration of this turn of events. It's the one and only, it's fucking Eve.

Lord have mercy, what is she doin' here! The Farmer screams in my ear.

"Hey you." I try to play it cool.

"Hey troublemaker" she's exponentially cooler to the touch.

"Where have you been?" I say it as I grin.

"I've had some time to think."

Remember that she's not trustworthy, she's a shady whore. Mrs. Bathory isn't a fan.

But she deserves to know what I've been up to.

#

I've told Eve everything. I even confessed to following a girl with the rudest intentions.

"I expected you to do that. You're such a player." She laughs it off.

"She was only to get out my frustrations."

"From our fight?"

"From you, the investigation, my mother's hearing."

"Wait your mother? I thought she was dead."

"I never said that. But, she's basically dead to me. She was supposed to be put away for life, after what she did."

"What did she do?"

Do not divulge family secrets! Mr. Solomon tries to prevent me from getting some things off my chest.

"She tied up her boyfriend at the time, while he was sleeping. Locked him in a basement and had her way with him for weeks."

Now ya done it. Farmer John complains.

"She sounds like a badass."

"She's not right. I was stuck down there for part of it. She was paranoid I'd run off and snitch."

"Fuck… you poor thing."

#

We talked about our mental illness. Illnesses, illni?

She told me how she was diagnosed bipolar with psychosis at age 13. That she has delusions which cause her to behave impulsively, erratically. She's been institutionalized for most of her life.

"I was passed around in every foster home and residential facility in metro Detroit."

"Why did you originally go away?"

"My parents basically got rid of me. They signed me over as a ward of the state. Lucky me."

"You must've been through a lot in the system."

"It was the usual physical abuse, neglect, and rape. Nothing new, nothing to write home about." She utters it so coldly.

"Dr. Kraepelin, my new psychiatrist, says I'm a schizophrenic."

"Because of the voices?"

"They…they fucking antagonize me."

Hey watch it, bub. Farmer John contests.

#

We're sitting on the roof of my trailer.

"Hey, sorry about throwing a knife at your face."

"I thought you missed on purpose."

You don't listen to us do you? We warned you that she's capable of anything. Professor Marks is wasting his breath.

"You're an idiot." She calls me.

Although I've been called an idiot most of my life, this time it's cherished.

"You're almost as crazy as I am." I challenge.

Yer not crazy, yer blessed, youngin'. The Farmer interprets.

"The fact that you believe that makes you more ridiculously hot." She continues to joke.

#

We both reveal that we haven't taken our medication for about a week.

"My paranoid delusions are back." she admits.

"My auditory hallucinations are so present." I try to warn.

"I'm also full blown manic right now."

"How does it feel?" I ask.

"Like I'm invincible and really fucking horny."

"The Board is what I call the people in my head. And they've been making me kill and cook people."

"Do you love it or hate it?"

"A mix of both. I'm actually good at this stuff. It's the only thing I'm good at."

You're that good because of us, lovely. You really should never forget that. Mrs. Bathory objects.

We're as certifiable as any other and one.

I'm the Nikola of torture, and she's the Hillary of fucking.

Chapter 23

The Whole 9 Yards

Eve tends to be the one who has the bright ideas.

She suggests that we go on a walk at the beach. That we'll both see if we meet something that captures our attention. Maybe a maiden, a group of able men, or whatever my girl wants.

We've driven my lemon sedan to Metropolitan beach.

At this hour, past midnight, the only people hanging out are those doing unsavory things.

She runs back to grab something from her jacket, which she's left in my backseat.

She's even cuter at night with darker features. Her wavy hair is black under the moon light. Her large eyes are shadowed with intensity. Those teeth from that devilish smile are bigger and brighter at this much later time.

We steer to the right once reaching the end of the sidewalk. We remove our shoes and I carry ours in both my hands. In her left hand is my black duffel bag of tricks. Inside it are the loyal shovel saw combo, shoelaces from a set of shoes Eve found in my closet, and my diving knife with a rubber handle to prevent what keeps happening.

Eve's jean shorts are riding up her ass, and the pearl colored beater she's borrowing are showing her side boob almost up to her nipple. Her small feet pin into the sand under us. I'm walking next to her, near her.

Have some decency, dearest and don't fuck here. It's in the wide open for goodness' sake. Mrs. Bathory kindly requests.

The first couple we pass is on a towel and making out. The woman on the ground is lying flatwise on her date. They're close to the streetlight. There are sets of people in both directions up and down the beach.

The next couple we come upon, are sitting facing to the water. They're smoking weed. But they're within eyesight of the first couple and it would be made obvious that they're being attacked. They'd likely scream for attention.

The third couple are both on their sides, making out on a large towel. The male character is over her missionary position. Both of their pants are up. They're dry humping. If someone is walking back from further down the beach, if they walk past us and disagree with what we're doing, then they would be able to blindside us. They could provide a lending hand to outnumber us.

We walk even further. We walk damn near to the other side of the lake. After the sanded beach ends. Into the grass almost into the campgrounds. We've walked past several trees, where it's dark enough to run into them. To make a fool of myself during this expedition.

We've passed a picnic bench and past that there's nothing in view.

"Let's keep going. The next one, no matter what, ok?"

"You've got it, babe." I'm finding myself once again following her lead.

The grass seems to never end. In the front of the park the dim light from the entrance of the campground is barely perceivable.

There's another bench approaching.

"Ready??" she prepares me quietly.

"Let's do it." I make my steps float in the air longer.

Without any additional words we're both directly on the path of the shortest distance between us and them. They are entirely oblivious that we're dashing toward them.

As we get closer, it's a woman sitting on top of her man. She's riding him cowgirl. I see Eve reach into her back pocket for something long and sharp. I can't clearly see what exactly it is. The blonde girl grinding on her partner is wearing a short skirt with her thong clearly showing. Her bikini top is pushed down below her small tits, rolled under to provide her more support. The guy's pants are still on, still buttoned.

When we're only a few feet away, Eve drops the bag which makes the metal inside clank. Both look at me since it's now closer to me than Eve. Not only did she not skip a beat, she quickened her pace to their side. She smacks the woman off to where her blonde flat hair is flung into her face. She then nosedives at his neck without giving him or her the opportunity to react defensively.

I do the logical thing and jump toward the girl after releasing both pairs of shoes. She's leaning back in utter shock, leaning against the palms of her hands. She's now sitting on her ass facing Eve.

My arms lunge at her shoulders, gripping her two joints and ramming her body back, banging her head on the hard surface.

Eve has a syringe against the young man's neck, "If either of you move I'll stab him in the neck and push my blood into your body. I have AIDS, motherfucker."

She screams loud but I hope not loud enough to apprise those back closer to society.

"What the fuck are you doing!?" the woman yells out of disbelief.

She's Lilith reincarnated. Mrs. Bathory proclaims.

Eve pulls her male victim down from the bench, into the dirty surface underneath. He's somehow on his stomach. Eve is pressing the edge of the needle in the back of his neck, right over his spine.

I rip off her pink thong. She doesn't kick. Instead she tightens the grip between her knees and turns onto her side. Her small neck the same size as Eve's goes into my left grip. The pointer and middle finger of my right hand go into her. I quickly push between her wet lips up to the last knuckle.

She shrieks, "AAAAHH! Oh my god!!!".

I look over to Eve, and she looks elated. She practically salivating while watching me finger rape this little tart while she holds her date down with a knee on the back and needle on his brainstem.

"Take off your fucking belt!" Eve commands the little man.

He quickly does as he's told. I know how that feels. But he's shaking uncontrollably.

She loops it through the buckle and places it over his head. She pulls on it like it's the reins of her very own human beast.

The girl I'm wearing like a glove, with now three fingers in her is whimpering.

"Oh my god, Austin!! PLEASE, please don't do this!"

It's become clear that no one can hear her. We have them in our restraint. They're entirely in our control.

"Ride my man, bitch!" Eve yells purposefully louder than her.

"NO!" her man dejects the idea.

Eve leans back while holding his neck harness, to cause him to choke and cease breathing. He's almost coughing.

I get on my back after releasing her pussy. Her throat is still in my grip.

She's pulled toward me and told to, "Sit on me, slut!".

She's weeping now, dry heaving.

She's sitting on me but stiff like a bridge, trying her best to not touch me with her bare vulva.

Eve leans over without losing her position to bury her hand in the black bag. She pulls out my knife to hand it to me.

I take the diving knife to press the flat edge against her pretty wet face.

"If you don't, you'll be the third pretty face I've carved off a girl this week." I coldly forbode the inevitable consequence to not performing.

She slowly pulls out my dick and packs her pussy with it. It's semi hard enough since all of this is happening so fast. But long enough to be penetrated deep into her.

The female victim begins grinding her pelvic bone across my lower abdomen while my dick slowly gets stiffer. It's becoming more enlarged as she's forced to fuck me while Eve is watching. While her man can hear everything, but barely see what we're doing just right above him.

I push the cold broad side of the blade harder against her pretty face.

Don't you go cutting the meat now. Farmer John warns.

I pull on her knees, "get on your feet and bounce on me!".

I look over to Eve, and she's masturbating while maintaining her knee on the middle of the guy's back. I can clearly see she's not only rubbing her pussy harshly with her palm, but she's sticking two fingers up her vagina quickly.

The young lady is crying uncontrollably.

A warm mixture of tears and sweat is streaking down her chest, over her nipples because when I try to squeeze them I lose my grip.

"Wha! Wha! WHY!!!" she's sobbing while riding and from time to time when she coughs her vaginal muscles tighten around my dick.

It's heaven on earth to see what I'm seeing.

She's lifting herself considerably in the air then sitting down with all her weight onto me.

She's ridin' you like a rodeo bull! Farmer John makes a fine comparison.

The man is cursing, "I swear to fucking god when this is all over I'm going to find and kill both of…"

But before he finishes, which was honestly a sensual scene that didn't need to be interrupted, Eve jabs the entire needle into the back of his neck right at the spinal cord.

He chirps briefly before expiring within seconds.

The bitch bucking on me bawls her heart out, "OH NOOOOO!!!! OHH GOD AUSTINNN NOOOO!!!!!"

When she reaches the end of her lung capacity she stops moving on top of me.

Eve stands up to draw out the shovel from the duffel bag. She swings it way above her head, like Thor. And snaps it down into his head, like an ax chopping at a stump. A chomp is popped into the space right next to us. When the bitch and I hear it, she jumps into the air, and from divine delivery her pussy muscles clamp down on the base of my dick.

I almost had a co-occurring heart attack and ejaculation during the climaxing.

Aren't you having a proper fine time, lad. Professor Marks comments.

Eve slowly removes the shovel out of his wet head. Spraying a bit of it on this bitch's lower torso, making her scream again.

"AAAAHHHHHHH!!!!!..." but she's intervened with my own blade.

Eve stepped over to us to grab my fist around the rubber handle with both of her fists. She uses it to slice open her neck. Right across the middle, making blood squirt out.

"GRRGRRGRRR" she gargling her own blood.

And I'm bathing in this bitch's warm liquid. I'm cumming maniacally into her cunt. By grabbing her around the waist I'm shaking her body into mine. Trying to cum as deep as I can against her cervix.

"UUUUGGHHH!! FUCK!!" I can't help but moan in ecstasy.

"FUCK YES BABE!!! WHOOOO!!!" Eve is so supportive.

After pushing out the very last drop of semen, when I don't have anything left, I push her off so that she drops to the side off the bench and onto the dirt. Where she belongs.

Eve walks around the bench and on the way picks up the shovel in both hands again. She stands square over the girl holding her neck as it's bleeding out. Eve swings the shovel way above her face, even leans back a little bit, and thwacks it back down with all of her strength. She practically slams the tool halfway into the blonde's head.

I'm still laying on the bench, out of breath, my eyes open wide to witness everything happening before me. My pants are still around my thighs. Blood is painted over my face, chest, and abs.

Now, don't you look like Carrie, except this is your party. Mrs. Bathory is enjoying the show.

"One more thing…" Eve whispers beneath her breath.

She walks over to me, and starts sucking on my dick. The bitch's juices haven't even dried yet and Eve is encircling her mouth entirely over me. She spits on my dick and breathes it back in. The blood on my body is smearing over her forehead.

She doesn't seem to mind. She's holding the base of my dick while bobbing her head up and down while slurping her tongue around my dick head.

This might be the best day of my life. It's a memory I'll dote on for a very long time to come.

We quickly jump into the water and help each other rub the slippery crimson ink off of us.

She's giggling the entire time, and I'm sure I'm smiling from ear to ear. It's almost starting to become uncomfortable how happy I feel.

"Hey Eve. You have AIDS?", I have to ask.

"Nah," she answers me while laughing more maniacally.

This is what life is about.

This is the sauce that not only adds visual appeal to living, but flavor to our wholesome relationship.

I've gotten away with burning down homes scotch-free. I've found my partner to carry out heinous crimes on men and women. She fucks like a pornstar. And I've learned to live with voices in my head. So that we all work together like a well-fueled death machine.

It's not what you know, it's what you can prove.

Chapter 24

The Inquisition

Eve and I didn't make it inside my trailer home. We've kept making out in the backseat of my cramped four door sedan.

We've fallen asleep in each other's arms.

She's in her panties and off-white tank top. I'm in my boxers and with my shirt off.

There's a knock on the window on which my head rests. Eve's head is on my chest. I slowly awake and rub the sleep out of my eyes.

I rotate my head to see what's waking us up this bright morning, and behind me are two cops.

They're on opposite sides of the fire marshal from the meeting in the Chief's office.

He calls out, "Mr. Strickland, please step out of the vehicle. We need to ask you a few questions!".

I push Eve off my cold body. She groans loudly.

"Who the fuck is it, Ryder?"

"Some cops with a guy from the fire department." I try to explain in as few words as possible to not alarm her.

She sits up and begins looking around left and right to observe what the disturbance is this early on a Sunday.

I slowly open my door and get to my feet after stretching my arms above me. "Ah. How can I help you sir?"

One of the officers next to him steps forward, "You can start by turning around and putting your hands behind your back."

Eve overhears this while she's looking for her shorts and gets riled up.

"What the fuck! The hell he's not!!!" She bolts out of the car and charges the officer making the arrest.

"Eve!"

"Ma'am calm your ass the fuck down!" he yells back at her.

This is just a formality. They're taking you straight to the Chief. Mrs. Bathory tries to calm us down.

"Let go him of him!! NOW!!!"

She swings at the officer and the other one throws himself into the storyline.

"Ma'am, you're under arrest for battery on an officer!"

I'm watching the fire marshal the entire time. I'm trying my best to analyze his facial expression. To read the diegesis behind his eyes. But I get nothing.

Looks like you done got got! Farmer John talks shit.

Eve is put in a police vehicle and I'm escorted to the backseat of the marshal's government issued car.

The sirens are bellowing through the quiet trailer park. The lights are spinning against the white canvasses of my neighbors. The commotion is causing people to walk out of their homes to watch us be taken away.

Remember son, there aren't any real consequences to being disloyal. Professor Marks implies that I should roll over on Eve.

But I would never. I don't intend on admitting to anything, but I sure as fuck would never blame Eve for anything I've ever done. Every body I've stacked or buried is my doing, on my own volition, of my dim imagination.

#

I've been brought into Detroit's Police Department through the back. I've always seen the front door, but I've been driven past a large fence with barbed wire. It's a sliding gate with more officers guarding every escape route out or road heading in.

With my hands still handcuffed on my back, I'm walked through a long corridor. Through several heavy doors only opened after a radio call to their operator somewhere else is signaled.

There ain't no snowflake chance in hell that you're running out of this one, chump! Farmer John seems happy to watch me be arrested.

I'm taken to a small room with a table and three chairs. On one end is a single chair, on the other are two. A small manilla folder is flat on the bolted down table. An out of date camera is on a tripod sitting in the corner.

We; myself, the fire marshal, and another unknown individual I've never seen find our seats.

Without delay the unknown individual introduces himself, "Good morning Ryder. My name is Detective Columbo from the Detroit unit."

"Mr. Strickland, you and I have met at your chief's office. My name is Deputy Paschall. I'm with the state's fire marshal office."

"Why am I here?" I'm going to keep playing it like I don't know a fucking thing.

"Well first we want to thank you for coming in. I know the officers and Mr. Paschall picked you up, but thank you for not putting up a fight. More making our lives easy."

They have no fucking idea how painful I can make their lives. How excruciating I can make it for them.

Don't think that they're doing you any favors. They're trying to persuade you by playing the reciprocity card. Mr. Solomon is finally giving me much needed feedback.

"You're very welcome, sir."

Just like that, my precious. You're doing great. Mrs. Bathory reinforces.

"You've been brought here today to answer a few questions about a fire that resulted in four dead. To be straight with you, you're a person of interest." The detective lays out the obvious.

"If you're straight with us then we'll just finish this as fast as possible and you'll be back on your way. We can have you back home as early as this morning."

Careful, boyo. They're trying to incentivize you. Professor Marks is giving me invaluable information.

"I'll answer everything that I can. I want to be of use to my engine."

"Fantastic."

"Great."

The manilla folder is opened and flipped to my direction.

"Have you ever seen this before?"

"Sir with all due respect, I've seen more burned down houses than I can count."

He turns the page for me.

"Maybe this will jog your memory." He points at a house, presumably what it looked like before I burned it the fuck down to the ground.

"I've never seen or been at that house you're showing me."

"Oh yes you have. You responded to a fire with Engine 34 at this very location." The fire marshal corrects me.

"I actually don't recognize it." that's not an untruth.

I don't hold the structure or bodies that I incinerate in any esteem. So I'm actually being honest when I state that I don't have them in my memory.

Keep it up, honey. Mrs. Bathory encourages.

The detective turns the page to another home. "Do you recognize this home?"

"No sir. Is that another house that burned down?" Asking inquisitive questions signals that I have no idea what's going on.

"You've got that right. Great guess. And this is the house after it burned down, we believe due to arson." Detective Columbo lays down his suspicion.

“That’s awful. You guys should go find the individual or group of people that did this.” I remark, absent any remorse.

“What do you think we’re doing here, Ryder?” Detective Columbo gets a decibel or two louder while pointing at the charred remains of the home.

The Marshal Paschall turns the page over the detective’s hand.

They’re getting impatient I see. Mr. Solomon makes a quality observation.

“These are the four bodies that were not saved in time from the fire. They cooked alive in the middle of the night.” The Marshal pipes in.

A good 30 to 45 seconds passes without anyone in the room saying a word, or moving a muscle.

Both sets of their critical eyes are staring at my facial gesture. They’re looking for any hint of response or enjoyment from what I see. They’ll get none from me. Because I feel nothing. I’m dead inside almost as much as the husband, wife, and two kids who were cremated by my decision.

They’re deductive approach is painfully obvious. Professor Marks is damn right.

“We’re also of the understanding that you were admitted to Eloise Psychiatric Hospital for hallucinations, is that right?” Detective Columbo sets the next scene.

“Yes, sir. I had a psychotic break, as I was told. But like I told you in the Chief’s office, I don’t remember much of it.” I stick to my well thought out story.

The homicide detective tries one more technique, “The report says that you were trying to spray down a house in the early morning before dawn. Like it was on fire it seems?”.

"If that's what I was doing, it makes a little bit of sense. Considering the shit I've seen. But unfortunately I don't remember acting heroic like that." I put them in their place while staring at Marshal Paschall as I assume he knows exactly what I mean.

Detective Columbo redirects my attention, "The thing is, it's a funny coincidence that you acted in the middle of the night, on an innocent family that didn't need you intervening. They were just trying to get some sleep, like the victim family!".

He's audibly loud now. He's too invested in this. He either loves his fucking job, or he's assured that he's got me colored, like a painting by numbers. But if I was at any real risk of being charged with any of this then I'd be in a cell already.

These motherfuckers are actually tryin' for a confession! Farmer John isn't as ignorant as he seems.

"Sir, sirs, I'm in the business of saving people from burning houses. I'm busy enough with school, my psych, and taking care of my girlfriend. I've never started a fire. I put them out."

"Speaking of your girlfriend, that you allegedly met during your stay at Eloise. Well we checked, and no one by the name of Eve discharged that weekend or the week before."

There's no way I'll concede to Eve being discharged on Monday. Because if I admit to that, then I'll lose my alibi. And show that I was available.

"Then maybe she has a different name I don't know about. I know her as Eve." I resent that they can just make shit up.

"We've also learned that you like to break the rules. You caused a campus wide manhunt and were found later smoking on the roof. Is that right?" Marshal Paschall has been doing his homework.

"We weren't smoking. I was getting my dick sucked." Setting the record straight would actually be in my interest since I already saw the line of reasoning he was beginning to set.

Detective Columbo intercepts, "So if you lied to get out of trouble there, why should we believe that you're not lying now?"

"I'm not lying now. I was afraid they would have extended our time of being admitted. Plus maybe I was embarrassed. I was a virgin when I met Eve."

Hey, easy on giving them too much information. Not everything is relevant. Mrs. Bathory redirects my responses.

Detective Columbo is quick, "Sure you were, just as I'm sure so was Eve." Both start immediately chuckling in my face.

They'll fucking pay for that one. I'm going to find out where he lives.

"Tell us about your voices. Do they ever tell you to do things?"

"No they just make fun of me, a little like you're doing now."

"Oh am I." Columbo challenges my assertion.

"You're insulting my intelligence, and my selflessness." I return.

"Did you know that the front desk girl at your very own psychiatrist's office has been missing since the very day after you met her for the first time." So that's the reason the homicide detective is here with me today.

We all saw it coming. Mr. Solomon would have been better off telling me that earlier.

"I had no idea, since I haven't been to my follow up yet. But she's not my type, I have a hotter girlfriend."

That was unnecessary. No need to add insult to injury, dearest. Mrs. Bathory is always on my case.

"Funny, you told your Chief that you had an appointment there yesterday. We checked. You didn't and you never walked in." Deputy Paschall tries to place me in an uncomfortable position.

My reaction at this particular phase of the interrogation is imperative. If I take long to think of a valid answer then it seems that I'm pausing to come up with a lie.

I quickly react on my feet, "I wasn't able to make it in as I planned. My girlfriend was having a manic episode. She needed me".

"So you're supposedly out of your medications now? Have you been hallucinating?"

"No I've been surprisingly well since visiting with Dr. Kraepelin."

"It seems like you've got an answer for everything don't you, Mr. Intelligent?" Detective Columbo is starting to catch on.

You see, stop being so darn cocky. Mrs. Bathory keeps at me while I'm trying to focus.

"We looked into your alibi of the arson in question. Records show that Eve went home the day after the fire was started, not before as you said you were *taking* care of her." Marshal Paschall gestures his fingers in air quotes.

"That must be a mistake. She was discharged on Saturday morning. I know because she was at my trailer after being at her grandmother's. You should go talk to her grandmother."

"Oh, we'll do that son. Don't you worry." The homicide detective emphasizes the part about me worrying.

But if there wasn't an ounce of truth that I was leaving here today, then there it is for the first time. They truly don't have enough evidence to detain me.

"Am I being detained? Am I under arrest for murder?" I might as well get it out of the way now.

"You're in handcuffs aren't you?" the detective stares dead into my eyes.

"You can be doing that because you two fear for your safety. You're scared of me." I look at both with a mild grin.

Didn't I just fucking tell you to not get cocky! Mrs. Bathory doesn't like this side of me.

"Son," Marshal Paschall leans over the small table "there's nothing about you that would ever scare us. Not in a million years."

"You're old as fuck. I give you another 10 to 13 years at best."

Detective Columbo leans in just the same but gets louder this time, "Is that a threat, boy!"

"Sure, why don't you write down that I'm planning a crime a decade in the making."

"This is a joke to you isn't it?" Columbo has nothing else to say but that.

"This is humorous that you would waste my time like this. I'm a fucking hero." I assert my purpose at these idiots.

Now you fucking screwed the pooch, you nitwit! Farmer John is yelling louder than all of us.

The fire marshal turns to the last page in the manilla folder, and sits back in his small chair.

"What were you doing responding to a fire in uptown, when you were specifically told to stand down until further notice?"

It's a picture of two small people, covered in black soot with carbonized bodies in rigor mortis. My hands are on both sides of it, but I only take a 0.5 second peek to not attract scrutiny.

"You ran in without permission! And you dragged out a man, while leaving his much lighter wife and kids!" Detective Columbo shows his cards, his true reason for speaking to me.

"It seems like everywhere you go, you leave a trail of bodies." Marshal Paschall declares what's plain to see.

Make a fist, son. Farmer John has my back.

I don't have to look down to become acutely aware of the bitch's blood fat still lightly layered on the tops of my nails. They're only moved under my palm while I make my point and emphasize on the victims.

"Next time, I'll save myself the trouble and sit and watch an entire family die. But I'm not built like that. I try to do my best, and I'm sorry that I didn't perform to your standards on that day." I put the responsibility of proving I'm guilty of anything in their hands.

"You really expect us to believe that, don't you?"

"I guess that would be my explanation if I was in your shoes."

"If I'm not under arrest, and if I'm not being detained, then I demand to be released."

"You sure you want us to do that?"

"You're wasting your time. And it's about to be more used up if I make a complaint to the IG."

How long have you been holding on to that card, son. Professor Marks almost sounds impressed.

They both look at each other.

#

I'm uncuffed and released out the front door. They do that so that everyone walking by can see that I've been held inside.

Waiting for me outside, is Eve.

Great, trouble. Mrs. Bathory complains.

"What happened, did they get anything on you?" She asks urgently.

"No, they're a bunch of amateurs. Let's get the fuck out of here."

"Ok, babe."

"Did they do anything to you?" I ask while walking hand in hand in the direction of my house on the west side of the city.

"I have an arraignment court hearing in 30 days. But since I didn't actually hit him they couldn't hold me. It's for a fine of obstruction." She giggles something wicked.

We're a team of conniving killers. We're bulletproof. We're indomitable. They can't get to us.

Emotional anchors manifest as reflexes to stimuli within the environment.

Chapter 25

The Ploys We Do On Our Toys

We stop by my regular dollar store to pick up some food. We've been going on for some days without any real form of caloric intake if you don't count swallowing each other's fluids.

I don't think she's manic any longer. She seems more undisturbed. Considering she was just put in the back of a cruiser then released to temporary freedom.

I walk in first to see if the regular cashier girl is working today. She is.

I can see from here that she's wearing the same tag. Her name really is Aria.

Eve walks in after me, as I hold the door. She also notices the girl immediately. And walks right up to her.

"Hi, honey. Do you any have any popcorn?"

What, is she fucking planning to watch a movie? Mrs. Bathory criticizes.

"Sure baby, it's on aisle 3."

I try to keep my distance from the conversation. I don't want Aria to be fully aware of my presence, or for Eve to get any slight ideas of jealousy.

Eve walks past me and grabs me by the wrist, "I like her. She's pretty".

I look back and the attractive cashier is staring right at us. I'm not sure if we're making a scene or if she's interested. I'm not used to being noticed, but it's a novel affair for me to be walking around with a beautiful woman.

"I see her every time I come in here."

You wouldn't let us touch the Philly, but now that she tickles Eve's fancy you're considering it!? Farmer John is pissed.

We're walking up and down each aisle slowly. I've memorized every product in the store. This is boring me to death and I want to leave as soon as possible. But anything for Eve.

"What do you know about her? I can tell you're into her, mister man." She calls me out.

"Not much. She's a good girl. And that she has a man, someone named Aiden, tattooed on her breast."

"That's not a man's name, cutie." She giggles while she murmurs near my shoulder.

She grabs a box of popcorn from aisle 3. And heads back to her new favorite cashier. We wait behind an old lady checking out with several cleaning supplies.

Eve is standing directly in front of me with her back almost against my chest. I can tell she's staring directly at Aria without moving a muscle. She's dead still and has observably slowed down her breathing.

Eve reaches back and grabs a handful of my dick. It makes me jump, causing Aria to look over to me.

She's so provocative it makes me sick. Mrs. Bathory is jealous.

It's our turn to walk up to the counter. The cashier smiles at us. Eve lets go and skips forward to hop right in front of Aria's line of vision. To distract her from me.

"Excuse me, would you happen to know where we can find a nice playground for our kid?"

"You have a kid? Um yeah… I sure do! But it's for little ones." Aria is taken aback but still pleasant as can be.

"Oh thank goodness. Ry is 6, and a ball of energy. We try to keep him busy but you know how that is!" Eve laughs like a mom.

"Oh my goodness, he must be the sweetest. I take mine to Victory Park." Aria is good at making eye contact with both of us and not lingering on anyone too long.

"You know what, we'll go take him over there right now before it gets dark. So you also have a little one too?" Eve asks with an endearing voice I haven't yet heard.

"I'm actually going to get my son, Aiden, when I get off. He's the cutest but wildest child ever. So I totally get what you mean by extra energy." she smiles at Eve and flashes her eyes at me in between.

They're both laughing like moms running into each other at the mall. Like I've seen when they unexpectedly meet and behave nicely toward each other.

"You should join us!" Eve officially invites Aria.

She pauses to think while looking at me, "I'm not sure, we're usually so busy most evenings".

"I get it. It's just that it's so hard to meet good kids Ry's age from good families." Eve lowers her voice to a whisper as if she cares if anyone else hears.

She glances over at me and widens her lustful smile. Appearances are everything.

She might actually pull it off. Shit, she ain't half bad. Farmer John gives his blessing.

"You know what, sure, why not? We can meet you there in like 45 minutes. Around 6?" Aria has the biggest smile like she's been invited to a holiday party.

"That's perfect! That way we can get little Ry some snacks before heading over."

Aria points at us, "Are both of you going to be there?".

"He's the best daddy in the world. He's always there for Ry, especially when we play." Eve is rubbing my shoulders while flattering me.

"Aw, good for you. That is a rarity." Aria and Eve are making sustained eye contact.

One would believe these two have chemistry, now don't they. Professor Marks observes.

"So you get off soon, and we'll meet you there? Do you need a ride?" Eve is noticeably sweeping her eyes down Aria's curvy body.

"Oh I'm good, I have my car parked back. Yup I'm off in 40 minutes, and we'll go straight there. His daycare is like 5 minutes away." Aria relays her itinerary.

"Awesome! See ya later!" Eve is sweet as you've ever seen.

She yanks on my shirt to direct me past her. I'm pulled while enraptured with Aria's facial characteristics.

Her hair is different this time. It's not in a tight ponytail, but down. It's half curly so it would be easy to throw her around with a well-twisted grip.

#

The moment we're out of the vicinity of the dollar store's view, Eve grabs me by the waist to whisper in my ear, "We need to rush home and get the car, and don't forget to grab the bag".

"Make sure you put the popcorn in the bag. We're going to need the energy."

"Oh and I have a special surprise for you!" She squeals.

It takes us another 25 minutes to get back to the vehicle in front of my trailer.

She rushes in after I hurriedly unlock the front door. Eve prances straight into the bathroom. She's giddy, and I enjoy watching her like this. She's in her zone, in her happy place.

I do this as a necessary evil. She does this to pass the time. I'm addicted to this shit. She suffers from a mood disorder where this is her baseline. We are opposites in that our atrocious behavior is fueled by a either a vice or disease.

You haven't the slightest clue about your wants. Mr. Solomon forebodes some bullshit.

She jumps into the heatless shower, I obviously follow her in. We take 10 minutes to rid ourselves of that blood, sex, and police car smell.

We take two minutes to get dressed for the occasion.

I'm wearing blue jeans and a white t-shirt. She's wearing jean shorts and a small t-shirt where her navel is showing. The idea is to be inconspicuous, to be as regular as a socially acceptable couple going to the park.

Another two for the popcorn to microwave. One to pack up the car.

I have the car turned on. And the duffel bag of tools in the passenger's seat.

Eve takes her fairytale time to reach the car.

"Oh shit! I forgot your surprise!!" she hollers as she doubles back to the house.

She runs back even faster. Eve buries some black object into her back pocket. When she shows me her ass as she sits in the seat, she takes it out. Whatever it is, she hid it between the seat and the door.

It takes us the entirety of the ten minutes remaining. We don't go past the speed limit, because being stopped by a police officer with what we have planned inside the front seat would surely put us in handcuffs.

We pull into the back of the dollar store right at 6 pm. We're parked in the spot facing directly at the rear door.

Right when I depress the brake pedal to its fullest length, where the car comes to a full stop, the door swings opened.

Eve turns to me "Put it in park, and when I give you the signal come out to help me".

Following her instructions is done without fully comprehending what she ever means.

I hope you know what you're doing here, lovely. Mrs. Bathory is always doubting me.

Aria steps out, holding her tired fatigued self up by the strap of her purse. Her hips are seesawing up and down visibly from the front as she walks toward us.

Eve approaches her from the side, causing Aria's facial expression to change from disinterested to puzzled, "Hey girl, you sure you don't need a ride?"

Aria responds to her approach while waving, "Hey…uh, I'm just parked right over there."

I can read out her lips of distrust. She has no idea that I'm but a few steps ahead of her, waiting inside the trap.

Eve turns her head, she's fixed right at the windshield. That's the signal. I open the door in haste and stand up immediately.

Aria looks over to me as well. The very instance we lock eyes, Eve punches her in the neck with a blue light, emitting from the snapping taser in her hand. Her brain is electrocuted for almost two seconds.

Aria's body topples and Eve plays catcher as she stops her head from slamming on the ground.

The lady has quite the reflex. Professor Marks gives praise.

I fly over to both of them. I pick Aria up off the asphalt, from under both arms. I drag her backwards as fast as my feet are commanded.

She's thrown in the backseat, and we jump back in so we can reverse to get back home.

The drive back is an exhilarating one. Eve has tied her ankles with shoelaces. She's sitting on her knees facing back with her chest on the front seat.

We roll through the trailer park as casual as possible, in no hurry. I park the back row as paralleled to the entrance of our home to the best of my ability. I'm too close where the door might not open.

Better makes this a quicky, don't want no nosy one's next door to see! Farmer John hurries us.

I walk out as slow as my body allows, and at a leisurely pace to the other side of my small vehicle, I open the door for Eve.

I'm on the dark side of the sidewalk where the devil and I meet. To discuss things obscene.

Chapter 26

Aria

After dragging in the unconscious body, she's released on the loveseat.

Eve rotates the limp body. She ties her hands together with a second shoelace. She walks over to my kitchen sink and pours herself a glass of water. Only to pour over Aria's pretty face.

Aria wakes up and immediately starts screaming.

Eve and I take a step back to watch her vocal lesson. She tries to get up after her duress has been ignored. Eve steps in to tase her throat to cease her screeching.

I like her sadistic style. Mrs. Bathory is beginning to come around.

We carry Aria over to the bed in our only room. She's thrown on the spring mattress, waking her up from forced sleep. The thin ties around her limbs keep her together like a log being piled on a truck.

Eve jumps on the bed after her, with the same infernal taser still in her hand. This time she rests it on Aria's crotch threatening to zap her genitals.

"Scream or try to run, skank, and I'll turn this on after I shove it up your ass!" The way Eve threatens makes her believable.

Eve is leaking from the face, but her tears are making rivers into her hair and down her cleavage.

I can still smell her from here. Her brown skin is coconut scented, with hints of lavender.

This harlot ain't goin' anywhere anytime soon, son. So take yer time quarterin' this here animal. Farmer John is indisputable.

"Why are you doing this to me! My son! Di…Did you make all of that up?!" Aria is reasonably confused.

She's jittering and trying her best to catch her breath. Eve powers on the taser dangerously close to between her legs, making Aria have a little accident.

"Oh my fucking god! She's pissing herself, babe!! All over your bed!!!" She yells while pointing her finger in Aria's face.

She powers the light between the metal prongs of the non-lethal weapon again. Almost into Aria's face. Making her tinkle light drops of urine on her khakis again.

I march into the bedroom and slither toward Aria.

"You need to take your pants off, bitch." I inform her while I whip out my diving knife to poke a hole under the belt seam. I stab her pants while holding it, and cut ąway from her.

Standing on the bed, I pull her pants upward by both sides around the hips. It rips down the pant leg folding Aria's legs up in the air. She flops down like a bag of meat.

Her shirt is cut off as well with the knife, and pulled away from her violently. The bra splits in half from being yanked in one hard movement.

"Yeah baby!" Eve has her hands in the air cheering while standing in the small space on the side of the bed.

Her ripped clothes are thrown down the hall. I step over her thick body so that it's between my feet.

"Open your fucking mouth, Aria."

She doesn't close her eyes. She just holds herself while laying on her back, spreading her mouth open half wide.

"WIDER!!!"

Eve is snickering.

With about one third of pink tongue sticking out past her lips, her perfectly lined teeth are showing.

I gather as much saliva that my mouth can accumulate. I breathe in sharply while puckering my lips. And spit a fair amount right down her trap, into the hole deep.

Aria immediately starts to choke, but transitions quickly to crying. She's whimpering intractably. Like she's being humiliated.

That's the way to make a gal fall for you, my sweet. Mrs. Bathory is behind me.

"Take off your panties, now. Because I want to see that beautiful pussy." I command Aria.

"Eve, baby. Get fucking naked please." She's told what to do, and does it.

Aria slowly removes her distressed panties. She anxiously places her hand over her crotch.

“Fuck her, Ryder. Fuck her brains out!” Eve has her back against the trailer wall. Now butt ass naked standing there like a barbie doll.

I grab Aria’s face once again, “Open your pretty mouth wide or I’ll break your jaw this time”.

“WOOO!” Eve hollers.

Aria is crying, “wwwwaahhh, uuuhhhh”.

But at least her sweaty face is taken over by her wide open mouth. I spit another ball of saliva in her mouth and some of it lands on her lower lip. Causing her to immediately turn her body over with her ankles and wrists still tied tight.

“Ry…hold her steady.” Eve instructs before she walks out into the bathroom.

I get naked while she’s looking for something. I put my knee on her chest with half my weight. My dick is semi hard and leaking long strains on her stomach. She’s struggling to breathe.

“Pa..pa…please don’t do this.” She’s already begging this early.

Like a well composed symphony to one’s ears. Professor Marks is enchanted.

Eve returns and bounces on the bed, “Ok don’t let her move, babe.”

She sits on Aria’s lower abdomen, compressing away any chance that she’ll jolt around or breathe in fully.

With a sewing needle in her two pink fingers, she grabs a handful of Aria’s soft breasts. Aria tries to see what’s happening by lifting her head.

Eve stabs the silver needle painstakingly slow through Aria’s right nipple, causing her freak out.

"AAAAAHHHHHH!!!!FFFFFFUUUUCK!!!!!"

"Hold her down!"

Eve grabs the other breast with more aggression this time and repeats the process with another needle. She doesn't act as careful since Aria is bucking around like a bleeding heifer. The needle stabs one side of her nipple, making Eve pop her body and almost throw both of us off.

"OOOWWWW!! NOOO!!!"

It doesn't go all the way in, so Eve removes it and stabs it again to make sure the ball of her nipple is sitting in the middle of the straight metal rod.

"Look at that, she's barely bleeding." Eve is eyeing her proud work.

We both get off Aria simultaneously. She's looking down at her pierced breasts, rolling around in agony from side to side, unable to get on her stomach as to not put pressure on them.

Eve comes back with a leather belt that was looped in my pants. She starts whipping Aria repeatedly.

"Get on your knees!!" she orders Aria.

She's on her fifth whip. Aria has rolled on her stomach to avoid being whipped in the face. She's crying.

"AHH!! NO! PLEASE!!!" she screams with each lashing.

Out of pity almost, I grab Aria by the hair and drag her off the bed facing down. She's thrown on the floor, where her body plops from hitting the carpet.

With her thick strands of hair still wrapped in both of my hands I pull her up on her knees.

"AAAYY!!!"

"Stay the fuck still!!" I yell while standing over her.

Her balance is weak from barely holding herself straight on her knees with her hands and ankles still tied like a hog.

Without command or forewarning I force my now hard dick into her teeth. She reluctantly opens her mouth to barely let my thick head in.

I reposition my footing. I move my grip from the top of her head to two thick grips of hair over her temples, right above her ears. Most of my erect dick is out of her perfect mouth.

So I jam it down her throat while yanking her wet head into me. My pelvic muscle slams against her nose. She instantly starts gagging. Her neck muscles are trying their damndest to go the other way, away from me.

I pull out fast so she doesn't throw up all over me. And jam it down her esophagus again, this time twice, not giving her a chance to fully appreciate the first gag. But she starts coughing which increases the tension of trachea encircling the end of my dick.

Eve whips her back like a slave mid-gag.

"AHHH!! Na! NO!!!" I don't let her finish before cramming the entirety of my rock hard cock down her breathing tube.

I'm holding it in deep this time. The revolting pre-vomit movement her neck is doing is making it delicious. The veins in her neck and forehead are bulging now. Eve whips her again.

"Look at her! She fucking loves it!" Eve has a point because it almost looks that way.

"Grrrr…Grrrg…Grrgrr…" Aria is trying her best to not throw up, while intaking an ounce of air, and sit up as straight as possible with her hair holding up most of her weight.

I look over to Eve with belt in hand. A string of pussy juice is dangling from the end of her labia and down her leg. She's immensely turned on.

Well ain't that I great sight for sore eyes. Farmer John is also enjoying himself.

Each of Eve's lashes force Aria's back muscles to retract so that she arches herself up.

I rip my dick out of her mouth, and with it a stream of saliva pours out.

"No…please…don't…I can't…" she's out of breath.

Eve steps away from us again. She's on her hands and knees looking for something under the bed. She slowly pulls it out causing a lot of noise.

I don't stop. Another ramification of cramming my dick into Aria's throat and her nose is starting to bleed. The blood is falling into her upper lip. Her mouth is also being filled with salty tears from her eyes. The spit hanging from her chin is now ruby red.

I pull out to lean over her. I stick my tongue in her mouth to taste what she's tasting. Just as I expected, a mix of her delicious saliva with the bitterness of sodium and iron from the orifices on her face.

Eve is carrying an old dog crate I had stored away under my bed, from my childhood when Mother once brought me a dog from the pound. Her ex stabbed it with a cattle-prod enough times that it expired in that very same metal cage.

She sets it up in my living room. It's big enough for a medium sized animal.

After that long kiss Eve lasso's the belt around her neck. Before I was going to get three more thrusts in.

"OH MY GOD!! NO! NO!!!!" Aria starts screaming once she's being tugged down the hall with her legs holding part of her weight up dragging on the carpet.

The kennel door is open. Aria is released right at its small opening.

"CRAWL IN, SKANK!!!" Eve looks more pissed now.

Aria refuses. I'm still in the room watching all of this unfold, stroking my shaft with the fluids left by Aria's face.

She gets tased on her back. Causing her to fall forward against the metal crate. Her limbs being tied together makes her stumble over to her side. Eve lifts body part by part to push Aria through the metal hole of the cage.

"PLEASE…PLEASE…I'll do anything!" she pleads.

I walk over to sit on my favorite chair. Fully naked I spread my legs so I can rub my dickhead while watching my girl work.

Once Aria is fully inside the steel crate, the door is swung shut and closed with the latch.

Eve turns the radio to heavy metal. Playing "We Are Chaos" – Marilyn Manson all the way turned to an ear-piercing level.

She sits her tiny ass on top of it with both pencil legs dangling on each side.

That dog kennel entirely slipped our minds when we originally planned this out for you. Professor Marks sounds surprised.

She's playing with her pussy inches above the restricted space in which Aria is laying in the fetal position crying. Eve is staring down at her shivering body while rubbing her clitoris in circles.

"We're going to fucking kill you, slut! But not until we've fucked every hole in your body!!!"

Seeing Eve like this is the sexiest thing I've ever seen in my life. Just when I thought her anger and confidence couldn't be any more impressive, her sadism is showing. She's thoughtfully vicious.

But I stand corrected because my pervert of a girlfriend starts letting go of her own fluids. A waterfall of urine is pouring down on Aria's naked body.

"Wha…Wha…What the fuck!!!" Aria is slowly starting to realize her dilemma.

That she's locked in a metal cage with her wrists tied behind her back and feet restrained to where she can barely crawl. Her face is starting to bruise, and the welts on her back are beginning to form. The liquid droplets on her skin are a mix of hers and our own bodily liquids.

Eve and I are making eye contact while this is transpiring. There's something romantic about getting lost in your lover's eyes while masturbating to a helpless body between you. It's chemistry in its rawest form.

Y'all are like two black peas in a trailer pod. Farmer John is now a poet.

I'm sure Aria can see the connection between us. She's watching our interaction with horror in her eyes as liquid is drizzling from the metal wiring under Eve's white ass.

Her face is mortified, whereas we're utterly infatuated with each other.

Aria hasn't stopped crying, and we're just getting started.

Pain isn't jealous, pain is sharing.
He's all knowing, telling away your secrets.

Chapter 27

Rape

Aria is threatened to perform for us.

Eve exchanges the diving knife for the longer boning one off the kitchen counter. She reaches into the steel cage and cuts the two shoestrings with one slice.

She kneels down to Aria's eye level. "Start rubbing your pussy or we're going to peel your fucking skin."

Aria turns onto her back and widens her knees. She starts rubbing her clit counterclockwise without the need to wet her fingertips. She's moist enough.

There's no moaning coming from Aria's vocal cords. Eve becomes irritated.

"Start moaning, BITCH!" She blasts both palms repeatedly against the top of the steel kennel.

"Uhh…UH…UH" Aria's moans are faked at best.

She's being demeaned. Being abused for our entertainment for a chance to live a scarce amount of additional minutes.

Eve leaps off the crate to break open the loud door. It vibrates the rest of the crate from slamming the door against the wall.

"AAHH! NO!!!" Aria is terrified of her.

She's dry heaving, panting like cattle scared of the upcoming slaughter.

"Come here, fucking skank!!" Eve has brutality coming out of her voice.

Eve grabs Aria's two ankles in the air. She hauls her out of the cage, milling the side of her thigh, ribs, and armpit.

I walk caboose to the train made of a gorgeous, sweaty tanned body. I can see her equally genetically-gifted pussy from here. The large, puffed lips the same color as her skin. The labia minora are smaller but suckable. Her clit is still hidden.

Eve lets her go onto her stomach in the hallway. She reaches down to the bathroom floor perpendicular to them. In her hand are my worn socks from days ago. She lunges onto Aria like she's a saddle. Her vulva is smushed against Aria's upper back.

"Ry, get me a…wooden spoon." She requests after looking around the room.

I retrieve it from a drawer.

Eve knots the sock to itself once around Aria's neck. It's almost as loose as it can be. She takes the wooden spoon and slips it under the sock collar. The stick is slowly rotated while bumping into the back of Aria's head.

It's becoming increasingly narrow as the sock strangulates her breathing. Causing her to make that straining sound animals make when they're struggling to breathe.

Her legs are kicking the carpet floor in conjunction to her fists banging the same.

I sit on the back of Aria's thighs, flattening the tops of her feet.

My dick is dipped into her scrunched pussy. Her thighs are fully together, thus making her lips squish against one another. I lower it and raise it completely out of her twice. Enough to lubricate it sufficiently.

It's slowly punctured into her tight ass. Inch by inch by inch through her.

She's now screaming behind her teeth, by grinding her jaw.

"RRRRrrrrrr!!!!" she squeals without opening her mouth.

The base of my cock is between the crack of her muscular butt. I notice Eve twist the sock tighter once again. Making Aria's legs straighten like two arrows. Her arms are stiff, with all fingers pointing out. She's trying to push me off her, but I'm obviously too heavy.

I lift myself up in the air and collide back into Aria's apple bottom. Up again almost all the way ejected out like a VCR player pushing out a cassette tape. Then rammed again to disappear my stonehard dick into her rectum.

Her entire body is knocking up and down. I can tell she's contracting her sphincter to prevent me, but I'm holding the base of my dick and leaning in slowly with all of my weight. She stands no fucking chance. Then all at once, her body releases. Every one of her muscles relaxes. Eve untwists the sock around her neck then swivels her body off.

"Fuck her even harder, baby!" Eve bellows.

My body is going quicker into her hers. I'm fucking the literal shit out of her flaccid lower body.

Aria all of a sudden regains consciousness and swallows in a gallon of air.

"NNNNAAHHHH!!!!!" she follows with.

Eve saddles back on, and starts to slowly twist the sock by rotating the stick clockwise again.

Aria is back to contracting every muscle in her body, including the one holding the skin around my dick extremely tight.

Eve is leaning her body back with both hands clutching the wooden spoon like it's a joystick.

Aria is barely breathing but I can see her head turning a hue of purple and blue.

After a forceful three pumps, she falls apart again. Her body going limp from blood not reaching her brain.

We repeat the process six more times. With each de-twisting of the stick counterclockwise when Aria regains like in her eyes, she screeches in pure misery.

"MY GOD! MMY GOD! MMMNNNNNNOO!!!!!"

Then stabbing her rectum with my stiff dick makes her lose her understandable voice to more of a throat call like some bitch in heat.

The radio has continued to powerfully shake the trailer home. I find my rhythm and beat to Rob Zombie's – "Dragula" playing ass fucking music.

#

After feeling satisfied that she's been broken in, we take a break. Some water on our faces to wash down the sweat from beating a bitch. She's senseless on the floor. Her spirit has been crushed into jagged little pieces. Aria is no longer crying but shaking violently from the adrenaline wearing off. The sock is still loosely around her neck.

I sit in my chair for fucking. The footrest is unfurled by pushing down the lever. The backrest leans to a comfortable position.

Eve throws water on Aria to wake her traumatized ass up. She's helped up with two handfuls of hair.

Eve speaks calmly into her ear while walking closely behind her, "You're going to ride my man, and your tight ass better know what it's doing!"

She's helped with getting on top of me. Her feet are planted on both sides of my hips. She's facing away from me with her hands supporting her weak body, so that she can lean back.

My erect penis is pointed to the sky while she slowly sits on my pelvis, making it insert slowly right into her anus. I let her elevate her body up over me and back down. She's not going all the way. There are streaks of blood showing on the middle of my shaft.

I get impatient. My lower body is thrusted up into hers. I want to feel the entirety of my penis inside her warm body. I'm stabbing into the meat above me. Over and over. Into her stiff body in a painful crab position.

I run out of steam and pull her in closer while crashing back on the recliner. Progressively I feel her asshole become ridiculously tighter. Something is being inserted into her vagina and it's placing pressure on the bottom of my dick.

I look down to see that it's Eve driving her hand into Aria's pussy. She's got her four fingers in.

"OOWWWWW NNN OWWWWWWWWWW!!!" She's wailing.

Rip her in half! Farmer John yelps.

Eve gets past the five knuckles and is pressing her four fingers around the base of my shaft from inside Aria's vagina. Slowly, Eve tilts her body forward to get her hand deeper into Aria's thick lips, up to her wrist.

Her five fingers are wrapping themselves around my pole impaling her asshole. Eve is squirming her entire hand from within her vagina. She's rubbing her palm and grip made by her digits along the entire bottom and both sides of my dick.

Aria's insides are tense as her sphincter is a tight ring around the start of my shaft. The middle and head are being massaged from the other side of the skin wall dividing her ass from her pussy.

The sock is pulled back with my fist within it behind her head. She's clearly in excruciating pain as her arms are trembling.

"AAAHHHHHHHHHHHHHH!!!! GAHD PLEASE!!!!!"

Eve is laughing her little heart out.

He's like a composer to a symphony of women. Mrs. Bathory sings my praises to the others.

Eve is punching into Aria's cervix harder and faster. Her grasp through the skin inside Aria is being grinded against. Her other hand is grabbing her by the top of her head, the hair above her forehead.

Her body heat is radiating. Sweat with other fluids are dripping on my chest.

Eve rips her hand out of Aria's genitals then returns with an open handed smack right on her outer and inner lips.

"FFFFFUHH!! FFFFFUUUCKK!!!" Aria squeals like a worthless pig.

By the roots of her hair, Aria is yanked off me and dragged back into the room. Their bodies are crashing into each other and clashing into the hieroglyphs on the walls.

Eve thwacks her wet hand into Aria's face. She smears the juices across her anxiously hot face.

Eve is stern with her instructions, "lay still and spread your stupid pussy, you little slut".

The taser is pressed against Aria's right breast, and the needle is cross between the two electric prongs. Eve turns on the electric power, making Aria jolt in extreme pain.

"NNNNNAHH!! MMY FFGGGAHH!!!!"

I climb over to her while her body is jumping around on the bed.

In one of her jounces, I hold her down to stick my dick in her vagina. Her legs are rocking on both sides of me. I slowly grind on top of her. Her face is looking away from me.

She's a fucking mess. Tears, blood, sweat, spit, and some cum painted on her face.

Surprising both her and me, a similar sensation as before while I'm inside it. She's fucking jacking me off from inside Aria's front hole.

It's incredulous, indescribable. What my body is undergoing must be one of the rarest sensations, not allowable to regular man.

Just as I'm about to bust and cum all over Eve's small hand, a knife out of my right visual field flies across. It land into the side of Aria's neck, and it's shoved all the way through. One carotid artery is severed from an outer puncture wound followed by another artery sliced in half from the inside. One smooth movement abruptly makes blood flood out onto my face, all over

Aria's upper torso. When I turn to the right to find the origin of the now perceivable boning knife, Eve is holding it by the handle.

Just then I ejaculate. My dick exits all of the semen being held back. I cream deep into her contracting vagina while she exsanguinates from outpouring blood. I convulse for some time while on top of her. Her eyes are looking past mine as she releases her last breath. Aria's mouth is agape in shock, but she's never looked more attractive. Her death being carried out while under me, while I used her body, was beyond poetic. It's heavenly.

I roll over to enjoy the transcendent moment. My diaphragm is contracting and rising.

Eve starts sucking me dry.

Right as the radio has changed it to "Down With The Sickness" – by Disturbed.

She's licking my soiled dick like an ice cream cone. Her tongue travels down around my balls. Sucking them like hard candy. She slimes her way down my grundle to where I can feel her breathing her nostrils against my genitals.

Her face is becoming more glossed with fluids of several colors. Her hair has red splatters intertwined within.

She's not here with me. She's still in a trance and now licking the meat off her bone, like a lioness.

She's wilder than me. Carnal like an animal from hell.

After sensitivity has reached its maximum toll, I writhe away from Eve.

I get up, "I need some water".

She lets me go but not without purring.

Right as I reach the hallway I hear something more terrifying than anything Aria has seen today.

I wane my head into the living room, to see through the window what's outside on the other side of the street.

I've been found and I'll be tried. For what I did to her.

There isn't enough time to rid the evidence off her body. No amount of ammonia, vinegar, or pliers will hide who she is.

A girl kidnapped, raped, tortured, and executed is a life sentenced.

There's no going back, there's only forward. What's done is done. She won't come back, her family is forever without.

What use is it to anyone for me to be taken away?

Instead why not use that potential energy to other resources. To finding other perpetrators doing worse things to more important people.

She died a useful death. For turning us on she was rewarded with being put out of her misery.

She's now in a better place.

The ethical question of change is a double sided dagger with spikes around the handle.

Chapter 28

A Moral Dilemma

Two police vehicles just pulled into my neighbor's driveway. A small team of uniformed men step out with their hands on their sidearms.

I have literal seconds.

The glass in my hand is half full. I chug it down to replenish my thirst. I'll need to feel refreshed for evading them quick.

Walking back to the room where Aria's manslaughtered body is swimming in a pool of her still warm blood, Eve stands up to walk toward me.

"Babe, are you going to use the bathroom?"

"No, it's all yours."

I stand to the side to let her pass by. I want to watch her enter the bathroom away from the trailer's entrance.

After wiping my chest and face of the waxy red material, I grab a clean shirt, the same pants, and a hat.

The singular window of the bedroom is just wide enough to allow my torso through. I slowly pull on the blinds to not make any detectable noise. I push up the glass and try not to slam or knock anything over while I silently jostle myself out of the guilty room.

To reach liberty from conviction requires you've got to want it bad enough. Mr. Solomon thinks he's motivating me.

When my body is halfway out, I see the lights spinning against the inside wall. Followed by loud bangs on the other side of the front door.

That was a quick pivot, to where they've been redirected at my very doorsteps.

As my foot is the last thing to be carried over the windowsill, I see the bathroom light emerge in the hallway from this side of the room.

Eve walks out and turns toward the light instead of to the right, to catch me mid-escape.

"BAAABE. We've got a problem!" she calls for me still believing I'm in the bedroom with Aria's unalive body.

We is too many. Now that I'm fully out of the house in question. I run off and find a hiding spot near a dumpster.

Eve is being hauled out of the trailer home, and walked down the front stairs in handcuffs. She's under arrest, this isn't some bondage game. Yet, she's smiling. Laughing out loudly.

"We found her like that I swear! She was already stabbed when I grabbed her!!" she tries to explain away the perplexing scene of the alleged crime.

As soon as the back door of the police vehicle is shut after her entrance, my phone begins to vibrate in my pocket. I have to find a distance further back to answer it. It's the hospital in Cleveland.

Behind a concrete wall, the phone is clicked on.

"Hello?"

"Hi Ryder Strickland, this is Mr. Addams from Newburgh Hospital." He calmly greets me and introduces himself.

Ya better keep yer cool, and not tip em off, now! Farmer John exerts his warning.

"Yeah, what's up?" I need him to cut straight to the chase.

"Sir, we've had to move the hearing up. Aileen seems to be pulling through. We asked for an expedient trial just in case her health deteriorates further."

That woman is impossible to kill. Mrs. Bathory dictates.

"When's the fucking hearing?"

"It'll be tomorrow. At 9 am."

I quickly think of the situation with Eve. How she's going to take the heat for what we did to Aria. The body is found inside my very own house, passed down to me by my mother. It's only a matter of time until they find out where I am or where I'm heading. I'm unsure if I'll be able to make the hearing in time, or how to get there three hours away. My hand-me-down car is in front of the trailer, with police now searching through it to find any exhibit of a clue to where I am.

"I don't have a way to get there anymore. My car has been…totaled." I try to explain without burning this bridge or alerting them that I'm unavailable.

"We can pick you up, if you'd like. The drive isn't that bad. Hey, it gets us out of the office." He tries to pretend that he's unbothered.

He's actually motivated to make this thing work. It's his job. My responsibility is trying to stay out of captivity.

"I can make it if y'all come pick me up." I lie through my teeth not expecting to be here when they show up.

#

I've walked along the back of buildings and down dark alleys. It's a challenge to stay out of the public view. Its disconcerting that maintaining my freedom is significantly less probable if the PD releases pictures of me. Although I don't know where or how they would find such images of someone like me. I know Mother never kept photos of us, and I certainly don't have any copies of photos of me or her.

In the middle of dumpster diving behind a KFC restaurant, my phone rings again.

What they gone and move up the hearing to today?! Farmer John complains.

I answer without reading the caller ID, "Yeah, what now?".

"Baby?" It's fucking Eve.

"Uh…yeah?"

"Where did you go, Ry? They fucking took me." She's sad on the other end of the line.

She's keenly aware that I abandoned her. We always joked that if we ever got apprehended we'd be the next Bonnie and Clyde of Detroit. We'd be national news famous.

"I got out, just in time." The best way through this is to be honest.

But I'm fully aware that the conversation and even my location are being recorded. I need to hang up on her right now.

"They think I wasn't the only one. They're looking for you, baby."

Is she insinuating that you should turn yourself in?! Mrs. Bathory is becoming irate.

"They won't find me." I deflect whatever implication she's trying to put on me.

It's an irrefutable certainty that if I walk into that police department where Eve is being held, than I'm looking at life imprisonment. We kidnapped, fucked, and tortured that girl until her death rattle. She shook turbulently while her air and blood exited her body's vesicle simultaneously until the life in her big brown eyes perished.

The scratches lined all over her body, interrupted by large welts over the bruising skin, are sufficient evidence that we did things to her entirely against her will. She was our slave and we the masters. The hunters that were minutes away from butchering her meat for easier disposal.

Eve knows this. I know this. Because it was all part of the plan.

"If you don't turn yourself in, baby, then I'm going away for life without parole. They're going to release my face to the news vans outside. They said the judge is going to make a martyr out of me. I'm fucking scared, Ry." She's playing on my heart strings.

I have the strangest gut feeling that there are officers listening in on our conversation. I can almost hear their incompetent faces wheezing on the line.

“I’ll think about it.” I try to hang up, without allowing her a chance to rebuttal. She could convince me to give myself up if I spend enough time on the phone with her.

But just hearing her voice start again, I’m captivated to hear what she has to say.

“Baby, I’m being arraigned at 10 am. You need to come here to tell them it wasn’t all me. They said we would be charged down the middle. We’d share the responsibility, the um…burden of the crime the detective said.”

To interpret what she’s saying as factual or her cunning personality is a task out of my wheelhouse.

Don’t you give it the slightest consideration, ol’ boy. Professor Marks chimes his caution.

#

It’s the early morning.

I found a way through the night, by way of an unlocked abandoned car with a blanket not large enough to hide all of me. I exit the aluminum shelter and stretch out my muscles before making it on the run.

Gradually, I’m finding my way to the next destination.

Unassuming is the key to staying out of it. Yet, presume that you’re minutes away from being restrained. Mr. Solomon pontificates.

Waiting at a laundry mat across from the dollar store is the safest point to watch for oncoming officers of the law. It’s also unfortunately the busiest establishment within a two miles radius. I don’t need Eloise staff questioning what I’ve been doing or where

I've been. It blends into the urban landscape but not frequented by criminals, hence not frequented by the police.

I've decided to go see Mother. I have a duty to that malevolent woman.

Whatever the sum of the torment she's passed down to me is, it can't be more than what I'm indebted for my abilities.

I'm self-preserving, therefore not willing to surrender myself for solidarity with Eve. She was caught, I was not. She'll do time with or without me. I'll do definite time if I confess. I have a chance to flee further and further from being detained.

I have just one last thing to do.

#

I'm again escorted by Mr. Addams and Mr. Erickson past security, through several different halls than the last. It was a quiet ride, and I had enough on my mind than having the effort to answer they're snooping questions.

They've walked me to a room where a long table is lined with three individuals in suits on one side. A metal chair is open for me to sit on the other side of them. A few officers are sat on the far end of the room, whispering to each other. The two caring men sit on the other end, to join several other individuals in civilian clothing.

"Everyone, this is Ryder Strickland, Aileen's boy. He's got a few words to say on the matter. Young man, can you tell us what type of person you know Aileen to be?"

"I was told to tell you all the truth. Or what I know to be true about the woman who raised me. She was a miserable woman who fucked me up and everyone else up, who got too close."

"Can you tell us what you mean by too close, Mr. Strickland?"

"Aileen was so fucking mentally ill that if you started to be around her too often then she'd start to turn on you. She would become delusionally obsessive on what I or anyone else was doing to get at her."

"Are you saying she was insane during your youth?"

"I'm saying that she was not only paranoid that people were following her, but she was known to be sadistic in her safety measures."

"I'm not sure we're following, Mr. Strickland. Was she unsafe or excessively safe in her treatment of you?"

You're losing them you nitwit. Farmer John scolds.

"She knew how to physically and mentally fuck me up, and make damn sure I could never say anything to anyone."

"How was she able to do that, son?"

"By setting up scenarios that were lose-lose for anyone that was targeted by Aileen. She'd wake up at 3 am to break my ribs since she believed there was a listening device implanted in my chest. But the kicker was when her pimp boyfriend came home, because Aileen would start a fight and blame me for everything wrong in their lives. So naturally, he'd beat the fuck out of me. Covering up the broken ribs with broken arms or a broken cheek."

"In your opinion, was she crazy when she kidnapped and tortured Mr. Jackson for multiple days?"

"If you don't think she was floridly insane during that, then you people have no idea how to do your fucking jobs."

"Mr. Strickland, I have to ask you to please not use that type of language in our conference room. This is a gravely important meeting, and it requires your maturity."

"Look, I know why she did it. Because Jackson threatened her. No one gets to threaten Aileen and get away with it. So she caged him up like a pitbull. The more he freaked out and yelled at her, the more she cut slices of meat off. She uh…she made me watch the last half. I was sitting next to the cage when SWAT charged in. I saw the insanity in her eyes. She was on planet Venus."

"Thank you for your candor, and your time, Mr. Strickland." The suit in the middle closes the meeting with me.

You shouldn't seek out your mother. She'll twist this against you somehow. Mrs. Bathory is logical.

I need to say goodbye to her. She should know that I won't be contacting her for a long time.

That she was right. I'm just as she expected. A beast like her.

#

Mother is tilted in her bed between sitting up and lying flat. She's barely awake, and I'm disgusted that I have to physically nudge her to get this over with.

Before I can shove her shoulder to start this conversation, she rises out of sleep and looks over to me.

"Ryder."

"Hey Mother."

"So you came to tell them all about me. Somehow your complaints are going to set me free." She ridicules.

"It's done with. I told them a hint of all you did." I minimize so she won't be as mad with me.

"You look different. I've seen that look before."

"What the fuck are you talking about?"

This old hag always has some bullshit to say. Farmer John grumbles at Mother.

"You're biological father had that look." Her eyes widen as she sits up a little more. "Now I know why you came here. You've been overtaken, and you're running from your misdeeds, aren't you Ryder?"

How did she ever know, who informed her? Professor Marks is dumbfounded.

I lean closer to her face and turn away to speak into her ear.

I lower my voice and tone, "I've been fucking up girls with my girlfriend. And made a fire or two, with people inside".

She smiles and shakes her head, "Tsk, tsk, tsk. Like father like son. He ran off or ran into a train for all I give a fuck. But before he did he had a thing for raping women. He was a married man, but a little too consumed with me. I was the only one that accepted him the way he was, but he started to stalk me and wanted to be around me 24-7. So I disappeared". She finally explains who I am and what has gotten into me.

Your father was unorganized. You have us guiding you, my dear. Mrs. Bathory tries to redirect me.

"That's just it. I need to disappear."

"How bad is the heat on you?"

"Bad enough to put me away longer than you." I for once relate with her doing hard time.

"Then you need to change your name. I guess this is a better time than never to tell you…"

"How do I change my name??" Showing my curiosity.

"Your last name ain't Strickland. It's Rome. That's your father's last name. You were born a Rome, but I never used your original name at the schools. I needed that name to die the day we left, if we were to get away from him."

"So…the guy they're looking for doesn't exist."

"I always liked the name Mason, since I was a girl. But your father wanted Ryder. So I conceded. I called you Ryder, but on paper you're Mason Rome."

I'm a nobody. And all at once, I'm somebody with no record.

She can see I'm zoning out, considering the possibilities.

"Go to the Michigan office of vital records, and request your lost (air quotes) birth certificate. If you find your father, kill him for me." She directs.

"I won't be calling you anytime soon. I can't ever come back." I fall deep into her empty eyes.

She side grins, "Oh I know. That's why I'm telling you all this".

Good riddance, I always say. Professor Marks tries to deflect her denouncement.

"They'll look into you, and eventually find me. It'll fuck up your hearing."

"They won't find you because Strickland isn't my real name. The mother's name on your birth certificate is Evelyn Miller. I use my middle and mother's maiden name to stay away from your father." Mother's sinister cackle is hair standing.

There isn't much else to be said.

I stand up, turn around, and walk out. There's no need for farewells.

"Oh by the way…stop listening to that girl. Even though she's been put away the voices haven't stopped have they?" she halts me in my tracks right as I was reaching the door.

I can't turn my head around to see her spiteful smile one last time.

But I have to ask, "They're both and the same one?"

"It took your father years in solitary to figure that one out."

I make my way out of the facility.

I start walking west. Where there's opportunity for a reset of my derelict life, but not before I return home for some things.

This savage woman just relinquished my true identity. My reason for being me.

The legacy I've been given feels both freeing and heavy.

It's malicious to be this inspired.

I can actually do this right next time.

Those who mind never matter, those you matter never mind.

Chapter 29

Identity Crisis

It's still the afternoon on the same day of the hearing. The sun is beginning to descend, glowing yellow hues over everything it touches.

I return to the trailer, knowing that there are likely low ranking officers staking out the place right at this very moment. I run from behind at the fiberglass structure.

Slowly to not make any noise once again, I raise the window at my bedroom wall. I crawl in and make sure I don't break anything on my way through the tight hole, alerting my presence.

Stepping gently on the mattress where Aria was diminished is arousing as fuck. As it stirs episodes in my memory of begging and crying. Her blood stain is cold to the touch, but fresh with just the top layer drying out.

You shouldn't be here. This is suicide, dearest. Mrs. Bathory fusses.

"This is necessary. Eve and I put some things away." I control the situation.

I gather some of my belongings. The smaller knife thrown under the recliner chair. A belt. More socks. Some underwear.

A mother is always right. Mr. Solomon changes the tune.

I grab the last popcorn bag. It'll be the last warm intake of calories that I'll be consuming for the foreseeable future. The microwave heats it loudly. It begins to pop its aroma of melting butter throughout the trailer.

"She's right about my four voices being the real reason I'm in this mess." I clear up some misconceptions.

You should think quite hard if we're the only ones to blame. Professor Marks is ruffled.

My black bag was dumped into the closet after Eve emptied out the torture equipment. I pick it up to start filling it with new items. I find the roll of tape under the sink. A missing screwdriver near the hotplate.

"I take responsibility for what I did… for all of them. But I was definitely fucking influenced by you all."

Just us, really my lovely? Mrs. Bathory teases me.

"I know I'm fucked up, but you motherfuckers don't really help."

You know who was quite helpful. The apple of your eye, Evelyn. Professor Marks is being sarcastic.

"What the fuck are you talking about."

Now boy, what did your ornery mother say? Farmer John recounts mother's warning.

I'm trying to read the symbols written on my walls. They're script and too unpunctually hard to interpret. Eve's name is copied more than once. More than 100 times on each panel.

In my mind I repeat her phrase over and once more. Stop listening to that girl. It took your father years to figure that out.

"How the fuck did she know that Eve was put away?"

The wrinkles of your distorted reality are beginning to iron out. Mr. Solomon gives his premonition.

If the court allowed me to attend her hearing, without arresting me, then Eloise Hospital has no idea who I am or what I did. Therefore, Mother has no idea that we were caught. I only told her I did it with Eve. What did my father figure out while in solitary?

He must have surmised that he was more Ill than he was led to believe. Professor Marks adds his two cents.

There are two police officers pulling up their vehicle behind mine. It has yellow crime scene tape wrapped around it like a bow on a gift. They begin searching inside it.

But she's everything to me. Eve was with me at my darkest moments. Like my guardian angel.

Or your demonic possession. Mr. Solomon asserts.

"But…I… I met her grandmother."

No, you didn't. You were in someone's room, with some old lady knocking on the door furiously. Mrs. Bathory blows my brain away.

"When I was inpatient… in group, they included her." I detail with unbearable confusion.

That there was indeed a woman in their group. Now much uglier and older than you think, son. Mr. Solomon expounds to further break my psyche.

"She was right there, when the couple and when Aria got attacked."

Now why do ya believe that? Because ya felt her rubbing on yer dick, or was that yer little hand. Or you saw her strangle some guy, or was that you multitaskin'? You tend to hear many things, son. So what do ya really believe? Farmer John reveals himself for what he really is.

My vision is offset to different points in time of the last several days or weeks or months. I can't tell. I've lost my concept of time.

This whole time we were protecting you to keep you out of imprisonment. It's becoming glaringly obvious that we weren't helping. So Eve was sent to work against us. Against you, which is we. Professor Marks formally explains.

When Eve first flirted with me I was in fact alone. When she chased me around Eloise, I was just running on my own. Carrying out Brooklyn's parted body and taking it to my secret location required no assistance from some little girl. When we attacked that gang member, I'm the one that walked up on them. She didn't distract the officers so I could get away, instead I got the drop on them before they broke in the trailer door.

"Eve is our enemy?"

She's your mother's vengeance. Mr. Solomon edicts.

I'm standing at the entrance of the trailer home. Two officers are on the other side inspecting my car on the gravel. By running my hands around the door frame, I see it's been kicked open. It still closes, but the latch has been bent almost clean off.

Holding the door in place is its contorted shape lodged within the doorway.

It's time for you to leave, darling. Mrs. Bathory begins to send me off.

The phone calls! I pull out my cellphone. The only incoming calls listed are from two facilities, Newburgh and Detroit FD. I never called out to any specific person. But I dialed 411 repeatedly.

Every time I thought Eve called me, I must have carried out the motions. But I was imagining everything.

The two officers are getting closer to the trailer, looking under it and moving things out of their way. I crawl as lightly as my slender body allows across the stained carpet floor, to not creak or slant the trailer on its heightened foundation.

Don't go forgetting your much needed medication. Professor Marks prompts me.

"But…you do know what that means don't you?"

It means that you'll be in a better state to do what you need to do, my precious. Mrs. Bathory tries to prepare me.

I've reached my murky bathroom. Inside it is my suture kit still opened. I zip it up to throw it into the black bag as well.

"You all don't want me to hear from The Board again?" I struggle to make sense of what I'm hearing.

Lad, if you're to do this right, then you need all actual hands on deck. Not imaginary ones. Professor Marks professes.

The front door is being finagled with. The investigating officers are trying to force their way in. A kick to the door.

I have the bottle of antipsychotic medication in my hand. I just remembered that I threw another one across the distance of the home, back into the living room.

One needs to rely on oneself. Not on fictitious characters of his consciousness. Mr. Solomon purports.

You're going to require the utmost discipline to stay out of incarceration. Professor Marks gives his direction.

Go on and make sure ya stay out of jail. For all o'us. Farmer John gives his blessing.

I take a capsule in my hand before dropping the bottle in the black duffel bag. I crawl back to where the officers are close to bursting through the jammed door. I'm on all fours like a fucking dog.

It's not under the recliner seat where I always expect things to be. On my hands and knees I scurry to the kitchen area to lift appliances up to look under them, nothing.

Yet against a wall, wedged between cardboard boxes and a broken air conditioning machine, is the barely used bottle of brain pills.

"If I take two pills, double the strength to lose my insanity, right?" I double check with The Board one last time.

Now you're starting to get it, lovely. Mrs. Bathory encourages the departure.

I crawl back as fast as I can to the hallway. The black bag is lobbed over my shoulder.

Rushing into the bedroom, slain on the bed still, remains the cold pale body from earlier. Aria is there. She's just as bloody, if not more. Still on her back looking up at her god with her mouth unnaturally open. Her neck is brushed with dark red blood and swollen twice its size.

No one has moved her. She wasn't planted after being taken away.

If she's still here, then the two police vehicles were never here. If they were, the whole place would have been ransacked for genetic and forensic evidence. Surely, they would have taken her to the coroner for analysis. But here she is untouched after I soiled her.

That's a second chance if I've ever seen one. Farmer John calls it.

On the floor right below the window, next to the bed, is a grill lighter. From when I used to cook outside. Luck will tell if there's an ounce of lighter fluid left.

I click it and nothing. Shaking it violently as the door is being rammed makes the lighter more likely to work. Finally, a flame is snapped on. I lower it to the corner of the mattress. It takes not more than 10 seconds to transfer the fire onto the cotton mattress.

Aria's body and my genetic evidence inside of her is going to be melted. Her bones will stay, but not the stuff that counts.

Stepping over her and on the edge of the bed I spring myself onto the windowsill. Carefully but quickly I pass my body through, right as the door to the trailer home is kicked open.

"HELLO!" I hear a police officer call out.

As soon as my feet hit the gravel ground, the capsule still in my hand is tossed in my mouth. I swallow it while opening the second bottle of antipsychotic.

"If I don't have you or Eve, am I still a natural born killer?"

You damn right you fuckin' are. Farmer John says aloud.

But no more killing. Mr. Solomon reacts.

Keep us free, and we'll always be here with you. Hidden from your consciousness. But inside you. Mrs. Bathory says it differently this time.

"I'll never get caught."

Ridding myself of everything Mother has passed down required burning it all down. The house, the furniture, her memories are rubble now.

It doesn't take long to see the flammable furniture of my room light on fire. Succeeding it are the carpet, then the walls, to find their flashpoint. Mother's trailer home is ignited.

My feet move my placid body. When reaching the end of the trailer park I take once last look at the piece of crap. It's eclipsed by fire. There's a police car backing up. But no police tape around my vehicle.

Second chances are not a dime a dozen.
They're rare coins double sided.

Chapter 30

Alternate Possibility

Sleeping in a jungle gym at some empty park is easier than being locked up.

For what I've done and who I am, they would have tossed me into the asylum. Doubtful that I would be integrated into general population at county. The department of corrections doesn't usually take serial raping killers. We're put into solitary confinement, to be forced to deal with our multiple personalities.

We're only meant to be institutionalized, like my mother and father.

Instead, I've managed to obtain a seat on a greyhound bus. I stole a man's wallet in the station bathroom as he had his back turned while wiping the shaving cream off his face.

The voices have entirely desisted. They're no longer present with me.

It's a quiet existence. Living among normal people around me. I don't have an audience over me. I don't see people for what they are. So the thoughts are minimal and desolate. They're still filled with plotting to hurt people, but enraged.

The cellphone I was using had the battery taken out and I crushed it before tossing it into a trash bin at a gas station.

I spent as less time as possible at the train station in case the police department was ahead of me in trying to get out of dodge. The bus, the defeated people riding it, and me are heading toward Illinois. The route ends at a terminal in Chicago.

I was able to walk into the office of vital records, with fresh clothes to explain that I've been adopted and lied to my entire life. That I need a copy of my birth certificate to set things right.

The young lady at the reception desk was a young suggestible female. A white resemblance of Aria showed in her physical appearance. Her self-esteem was showing, and I took it for a spin.

She told me she's not allowed to ask for reprints without a government issued ID.

"I'm really not allowed to issue copies to anyone without a license, or some form of identification." She tried to tell me.

I told her I was born and raised in Flint. That being in and out of foster homes made it hard to hold onto any documents. Which isn't too far from the truth, although it was more Eve's truth.

Her eyes went from shielded to endearing in a blink. Mrs. Bathory always said, a disingenuous smile will go a long while. The trick was not to act desperate, but to layer my ask with injustice against a hopeless kid.

"Look I don't want you to lose your job. I was just hoping that someone could help me out for once." I licked my lips to distract her from the vacancy in my eyes.

“Um… I get off at 6. Meet me at the McDonald’s across the street. I’ll have it for you if you’ll wait for me.” She almost makes a decent conspirator.

She committed what I’m sure is a felony.

We met at the fast food place parking lot. She waved for me to hop into her vehicle. We made small talk which pained me almost as much as sitting around for two hours, surrounded by fat fucks who ate while I haven’t.

She handed me the folded certificate, but toyed with her hair while doing it.

“So I hooked you up, what are you going to do for me?”

She’s implied that my future identity was for sale. That I can work my way to freedom on her body.

“Just tell me what you really want, and you might get it.” I bluntly made her put her cards on the dashboard.

“I want you inside of me.” She looked down while saying it.

To save the suspense, I choked her out for a bit and made her cum with my three middle fingers. She sucked me half as good as Eve would. Her government worker mouth did the bare minimum, couldn’t deepthroat, and forgot to play the balls.

But, at least she swallowed. Likely because she was actually hungry, or starving for dick. Eve was never hungry for just dick. She was more blood thirsty. Impulsively dependent on fucking brains to death to feel normal.

But that wasn’t real.

This one is at least using me, whereas Eve was a self-defeating figment of my imagination.

#

The social security office was less demanding of effort than the birth certificate. My social security number has never been recorded. They found it strange, but issued me a temporary printed copy for now. The foster care anecdote is a winner with most people.

In my pocket are two fresh forms of identification, sufficient for a second chance at one last life.

With a driver's license from the state of honest Lincoln, the remainder of my dishonorable life will be carefully planned. It's time to do things right.

I'm going to have a normal life and a normal appearance. When someone looks me up they'll only find regularity, order, boredom. On the surface.

Beneath I'll find a way to let out my demons. The Board may have gone into hiding. Eve has dissolved into being a distant memory. The hunting skill The Board said I have will be utilized somehow. Eve's unquenchable hunger will be honored.

I need to change my appearance.

I go to a dollar store down the street of the station.

Hair dye, off brand Rogaine for a beard, and scissors to cut my hair.

Cameras will always be watching, so I need to play the part a little better.

#

The Chicago Union Station is a hotbed of colors, economy, and transient energy.

Walking around the station, through corridors, I embrace the overwhelming sights.

People of different means, of different races, are strolling around teeming with potential pain. They're prey that aren't from a small pond of low quality. But a sea of specimens.

My victim pool has been upgraded. These are real people with real things to lose and pay for.

I've already spotted three, now four, five prospective casualties. Women like I've never before seen. Some filthy rich, others with professional confidence, and so many fucking vulnerable ones.

On a tv news bulletin in a lounge is a hot female reporter describing, "a possible arson where a dead woman in Detroit was found after the fire died down. Initial coroner reports say she was tortured and dead before the act. The home belonged to a woman who is now in a psychiatric hospital, while her son, Ryder Strickland, is being searched for to bring in for questioning. A picture or description of him have not been found".

I've made national news, and the recognition strokes my ego. But that'll be the last time I'll savor any portion of infamy. My name, Mason Rome, will be attached to accolades and reputation.

My step is lighter in weight with the concern of being found removed for a while. I'm invincible among people.

To do this I'm going to need to evolve. I can't remain as me.

Pulling this off, the concept of being the absolute worst, is going to take a reinvention of the wheel. I need to become the highest form of tactician in creating art. In creating suffering for my insatiable taste for pain.

There's opportunity here on every sidewalk. In every building. In each establishment where I can handpick my selections on a butcher's block.

Immersing myself with these people necessitates credentials, reputation, and charming skill. The things I have none of.

Creating the opposite of me, while keeping my genetics, is going to take years. Probably a fucking decade.

I'm going to lie, cheat, steal, and fuck my way to the top. And stay there perched like a vulture on a roof.

This will requires the work of a psychopath. A predatory killer.

But The Board explicitly charged me with no more killing.

How the fuck am I going to accomplish this?

Like a professional would.

Practice.

Made in United States
Troutdale, OR
12/08/2023

15549721R00156